T0162626

THREE YEARS
LOST IN SPACE

THREE YEARS LOST IN SPACE

MARK GODDARD

THREE YEARS LOST IN SPACE

iUniverse books may be ordered through booksellers or by contacting:

iUniverse
1663 Liberty Drive
Bloomington, IN 47403
www.iuniverse.com
1-800-Authors (1-800-288-4677)

Because of the dynamic nature of the Internet, any web addresses or links contained in
this book may have changed since publication and may no longer be valid. The views
expressed in this work are solely those of the author and do not necessarily reflect the
views of the publisher, and the publisher hereby disclaims any responsibility for them.

Any people depicted in stock imagery provided by Thinkstock are models,
and such images are being used for illustrative purposes only.
Certain stock imagery © Thinkstock.

ISBN: 978-1-4917-9757-0 (sc)
ISBN: 978-1-4917-9758-7 (e)

Library of Congress Control Number: 2016908167

Print information available on the last page.

iUniverse rev. date: 05/26/2016

Dedicated

to

The Members of the

Mark Goddard Appreciation Society

(MGAS)

and all *Lost in Space* fans

Foreword

I've been a *Lost in Space* fan for a very long time. In 1974, my buddy and I turned a basement into the upper deck of the Jupiter 2 complete with painted styrofoam control panels, a Big Wheel mounted on a giant cardboard box as the astrogator, lawn chairs for our space couches and Play-Doh formed into the shape of the central radar display. I always played Don West. As far as I was concerned, Don West was the hero, the romantic, the skeptic, the anchor and the heart and soul of the Robinson expedition. Don West as portrayed by Mark Goddard displayed all those qualities week after week on *Lost in Space*. He was the perfect compliment to Guy Williams' swashbuckling and intellectual Professor Robinson. Many years later in 1989 while working at a local TV station, I had the opportunity to visit Mark's home in Scituate, Massachusetts for a one on one sit down interview. It was such a thrill to be actually asking questions to the person I had been watching on television for all these years. The interview took place one week after the passing of Guy Williams. As a result, our interview also became cathartic for both of us as we reflected and reminisced about what Guy had meant to us, for me as a fan and for Mark as a colleague and friend.

Fast forward to 2014. I hadn't spoken to Mark in twenty-five years, but, thanks to the Internet, fans can connect with their favorite celebrities in a way that was not possible back in the days when *Lost inSpace* was on the air. I, along with several thousand fans, got to reconnect with him and the rest of the cast. When the opportunity was presented to me to help Mark with the illustrations and photos for this book, I jumped at the chance. Mark wanted to write a book for the fans specifically about his three years on *Lost in Space*. His unique viewpoint on his experience as Mark Goddard the actor and as the character of Don West is what makes this a must read for every dedicated fan. I'm honored to call him a friend. From the fans of the Mark Goddard Appreciation Society (MGAS), the *Lost in Space* Classic Series page, the *Lost in Space* Memories page and the *Lost in Space*- Alpha Centauri Society Group, we say thank you, Mark, for the many enjoyable hours watching your exploits as Major Don West. May you keep piloting for many years to come.

Perry Corvese
Long time *Lost in Space* collector and fan

Grateful Appreciation To

Kevin Burns, who provided photos to be used in this book along with his unwavering support of this project. I salute and thank you, my longtime friend.

Perry Corvese, who not only designed the book cover but chose, placed, and enhanced the photos for *Three Years Lost in Space*. I'm thankful for his outstanding talent and his friendship. A thank you also to his lovely wife, Karen, for her hospitality during my visits to their home in Connecticut.

Patrick Tieng, my liaison at iUniverse, for his patience and valuable assistance during the creation of *Three Years Lost in Space*.

Ron Nastrom, for his wonderful and creative sketches. His talent is undeniable and his friendship is forever.

Introduction

A few years ago, I wrote an autobiography called *To Space and Back*. It was received quite well by *Lost in Space* fans although they had one common criticism. They felt that there was too little written about the series *Lost in Space*. I agree with them, but it was, after all, a memoir about my entire life up until the year 1997. Fans of Don West who are members of MGAS (Mark Goddard Appreciation Society) on Facebook were the encouraging factor that inspired me to take on the challenge of writing a book about my three years on *Lost in Space*.

There are many books and handbooks on *Lost in Space*, but besides Angela and Billy's photo book this is the only one written by a cast member. I wanted to write a book wherein the fans would feel I was interacting with them on a personal level about the show. If I've been successful, I think you will enjoy reading this book as much as I enjoyed writing it.

Contents

How I Got to Be on *Lost in Space*

Before I recall my *Lost in Space* years from 1965 to 1968, I want to share with you the circumstances that led to my being cast in this memorable series. If you read my memoir, *To Space and Back,* you're aware of my co-starring roles in *Johnny Ringo* and *The Detectives.* I was able to land roles in those two series through agent representation. In each case, the producer of the series was represented by The William Morris Agency. I was also represented by that agency, so I became part of what was known as a package deal. If an agency puts together a combination of talent that it represents for the production company or producer that it also represents, it is considered a package. Some package deals put together at The William Morris Agency were shows that were produced at Four Star Television such as *The Rifleman, Johnny Ringo* and *The Detectives.*

It went like this: Package deals were created by talent agencies. Tobacco companies or automobile corporations like Kent cigarettes or Chevrolet would be the sole sponsor of a show. Advertising agencies such as Benton and Bowles would handle the deal for the sponsor who would take care of the financial responsibilities. That's the complicated but factual side of how I got here.

Now, here is the personal side. With two series under my belt, I was feeling pretty cocky about my

Hollywood career. I was only twenty-six years old and figured movies would be the next logical step to my hopefully, meteoric stardom. Not to be. Going from acting in television to acting in movies was not a hop but a big jump, equal to being a star college athlete to becoming a professional athlete. Among series stars or co-stars, I can think of very few who made the jump successfully. Steve McQueen, James Garner, Burt Reynolds, Tom Hanks and Clint Eastwood are among the small number who became true Hollywood stars. In retrospect, no agency, no matter how powerful, could have made me a movie star, but I didn't realize that back then. So, I left the William Morris Agency and signed with General Artists Corporation (GAC) who happened to represent Irwin Allen.

Irwin Allen was the creator and producer of *Lost in Space* as well as other popular series such as *Voyage to the Bottom of the Sea.* It was well known that Irwin was pretty generous when it came to spending on sets and special effects but rather frugal when it came to spending money on actors. My personal opinion was that Irwin didn't particularly like actors and was more comfortable with explosions and inanimate objects. For example, he created an expensive set for the pilot which was later used for our initial show, "The Reluctant Stowaway." The impressive set with extras taking the parts of journalists, Alpha Control engineers, and military personnel, etc. was beyond what television studios usually spent on pilots. Equally impressive was the talent Irwin was able to garner for the series.

We had Guy Williams of *Zorro* fame. We had June Lockhart of *Lassie* fame. We had Angela Cartwright of *Make Room for Daddy* fame. Marta Kristen of *Beach Blanket Bingo* fame. Billy Mumy of *Dear Brigitte* Fame and last, but not least, Jonathan Harris of *The Third Man* fame. I might mention here that in addition to my earlier series, Jonathan and I appeared in *The Bill Dana Show* together. He was a regular, and I was the guest star. On *Lost in Space,* I was the regular, and Jonathan was the guest star. Oops, excuse me. Jonathan was *special* guest star. A well deserved billing which he devised and was agreed upon by Irwin Allen. Jonathan came aboard after billing for the rest of the cast had been settled by Irwin and the other actors' agents. Star billing was shared by Guy and June. Jonathan didn't want anything less than star billing, so "special guest star" billing suited him just fine.

I can't resist relating here the one time I got "special" billing over Guy Williams. One day Guy and I were on the campsite set, standing there after the rehearsal of a scene when Irwin came through the stage door like a mini tornado. He marched right up to Guy and called him a prick. As soon as he came in, I snuck behind a big fake boulder to avoid being seen by an obviously angry Irwin. It didn't work. He spotted me out of the corner of his eye, pointed his finger at me and said very loudly, "And you, Goddard, are a triple prick!" I don't know why he felt that way at this particular moment, but I thought to myself, "Hey, I got billing over Guy!"

In retrospect, even though I didn't have top billing, co-starring in *Lost in Space* was truly a stroke of good luck. But, at the time, my cockiness hadn't worn off, and I was reluctant to be in another series, especially one that would have me flying around the universe. My agent at GAC advised me to do it, however, and it would be another package deal. I was beginning to feel like a bottle of Jack Daniels in a brown paper bag, going from one liquor package store to another and yet another. But, I was about to trade in the brown paper bag for an aluminum space suit.

How Don West Got to Be on *Lost in Space*

Don was quite the nerd and yet quite the hotshot at the same time while attending college. He rocked in academics as a young student at a class A university and still enjoyed the usual activities that students were involved in like fraternity life and sports. His problem was that he spread his talents too thin and lost confidence in his abilities to juggle a number of things simultaneously.

Also, things came too easy for him, and he failed to develop the strong work ethic necessary for success. He dabbled in geology and then joined the Air Force so he could take pilot training. He became a shuttle scientist at twenty-three and then joined the Jupiter mission (once named the Gemini mission). He was selected for his talents as a scientist and pilot and for his youth and experience. Overlooked was his bent for aggressive behavior and his short temper. He was definitely looking forward to a mission that could change the outlook of space travel in the future.

Traveling with a family in space was not his first choice of discovering the secrets of the vast universe, but the opportunity of being part of this momentous expedition came up and was too enticing for him to decline. His excitement got the better of him, and he spent a sleepless night before the anticipated lift off.

But when it came, Don was thrilled to be part of Alpha Control's historic mission to colonize the far reaches of space. It didn't hurt either that a beautiful blond was on board to take his mind off the awesome responsibility for safely piloting the Robinson family to their cosmic destination.

Wardrobe for Space Travel

When I received the call from my agent to report to Twentieth Century-Fox for a wardrobe fitting, I had mixed feelings about doing this series. On the one hand, it was a job that would be paying me very well. On the other hand, I couldn't relate to a series that was set in space. But, I had an out, so I thought why not do the pilot and take the money and run, as the saying goes. What I thought was an out was only the word of my agent at GAC who told me that he was positive, "This series will never sell." Guess what? He was wrong! At the time I didn't know he was wrong, so in one way I looked forward to working at a major motion picture studio. "Who knows?" I thought, "Maybe I'll meet and be discovered by a real honest to goodness movie producer." I'm not sure why I thought that because I had met many of them in my personal life. But, I could dream, couldn't I?

Wearing sunglasses, I drove my blue '65 Fiat spider convertible to the front gate. The police guard, after the usual procedural questions, nodded me through with a gesture of approval.

So, here I was at Twentieth, not as a movie star but to get outfitted for a role in a science fiction pilot. The costumers already knew my measurements, so I went to the wardrobe department to get fitted for my space suit. Well, they put me into a silver jump suit with silver boots and then sent me over to a stage where they were ready to take publicity photos of me. I stood there and was about to cry, thinking of the high hopes I had of being the next James Dean, not Flash Gordon. The glistening silver outfit looked pretty goofy to me. Over the years, the unflattering and uncomfortable material was to become a point of interest to our fans. When we were asked how we liked the silver outfits, the answers were always the same: They were hot, they were stiff, and you couldn't sit down in them. I always said that I personally felt like a potato, wrapped in aluminum foil, ready to get baked.

It wasn't all bad, though, because it gave me comic material to use in my very first public appearance to publicize *Lost in Space*. I was sent to Agawam Park in Fitchburg, Massachusetts, a place I knew about. I needed to entertain an audience for about thirty minutes. I was asked to do a kind of stand up comedy routine, and this frightened the hell out of me. I asked my good friend, Buddy Hackett, to help me write a skit. Buddy told me that his material would be too blue for me to use, so he sent me to his good friend, the comedian, Jack Carter. Jack and I were able to put together some material, and I'd like to share one story I told to the gathering in Fitchburg. Some of it is actual, and some is embellished for entertainment value. I'll let you decide which is which. It went like this:

"Hi, everyone! I'm Mark Goddard, and I'm very happy to be here in Fitchburg. I did summer stock at the Lake Whalom Playhouse a few years back. If you're wondering why I'm dressed like this, it's because I'm in a new series that will be on television this fall. It's called *Lost in Space.* I don't always dress like this, but let me share a story with you about another time I wore this space suit in public. To say the least, it caused me quite a bit of embarrassment.

I lived on Coldwater Canyon drive, which leads into Beverly Hills. We filmed *Lost in Space* at Twentieth Century-Fox studios, which is a fifteen minute drive from my home. One day, we were filming a sequence in which I was walking in space, and I was wearing this space suit. During our lunch break, I received a message from my wife that she forgot my daughter's lunch at home and asked me to I pick it up and bring it to my daughter at nursery school. I hurried out of the sound stage dressed like this and took my space helmet with me and placed it, open end up, on the passenger seat next to me. I picked up the lunch, and as I was driving to my daughter's nursery school in my Fiat convertible, with the top down, it started to pour. As I was wrestling to get the manual top up, I heard the siren of a police car. I pulled over. The downpour ended as quickly as it started, and an unhappy police officer stepped to the side of my little Fiat.

"You were going pretty fast, don't you think? Where were you going in such a hurry?"

"Nursery school," I nervously answered.

"What are you majoring in?" he sarcastically asked. "Sandbox?"

"No, sir, you see...well, it's a long story."

"I'll bet it is," he said.

"No, officer, you don't understand," I muttered.

"I don't understand?" he bellowed. "I'm here with a nut job, dressed in silver lame pajamas with an empty fishbowl next to him, and I don't understand? Where's the fish? Did you eat the fish?"

"It's not a fishbowl, I tried to explain. "It's a space helmet."

"Oh, really"? he mockingly asked.

"No, really," I said. "You see, I just finished walking in space."

The policeman looked at me for the longest while before shaking his head.

"Why don't we try space walking to the station," he stated with a wry expression.

Well, we never had to, as things worked out. We ended up with the policeman escorting me to the nursery school where I was embarrassingly identified by the teacher. This was after my crying daughter refused to say anything, except when asked if I was her father, stated, "My daddy doesn't dress like that!" Yeah, well, tell that to the wardrobe department I thought with a bit of contempt.

The silver jumpsuits were unearthly enough, but that was only the beginning for the wardrobe department that received its orders from Paul Zastupnevich, Irwin Allen's right hand man. The planned wardrobe change, after our five and one-half year voyage, was to have us dress in something more comfortable and stylish as we began the colonization of outer space. Comfortable and stylish? Let me tell you, the costume department must have had a lot of laughs designing these outfits even though the show was in black and white. I remember wearing a red turtleneck dicky under a grey top that was as itchy as hell. John Robinson wore a red turtleneck under a square bluish grey velour shirt. Will Robinson had the best looking outfit. He wore a blue collared top, dark blue pants and black boots. The ladies on the venture didn't fare as well. Maureen and Penny were in mustard colors--Maureen in Grey Poupon and Penny in French's. Judy's wardrobe was the only one pleasing to the eye. She wore a red collared top, blue tights with a dark blue skirt and blue boots.

Maybe the first year costumes weren't as bad as I thought at the time but I certainly didn't like mine. I never said anything because I didn't think alterations were possible. I figured we were out in space and continuity of costumes would prohibit a change. Boy, was I wrong! I found out that Jonathan Harris changed his original costume which he wore for only three episodes. The outfit they originally gave him to wear was a dark brown velour which did nothing for his character. He later wore a beige velour top (all the tops for the male characters were made of velour) with a yellow turtleneck. In the third season, he wore a black top that better suited his villainous, comedic character.

I liked my second season get up better. I wore a rust colored velour shirt with a yellow zippered collar. It had two stripes on my right torso. One stripe was yellow, and the other was a dark rust. I had no idea what the stripes signified, but it was overall more in the cowboy line of attire which made me happy. It also made me somewhat nostalgic for the days of westerns.

I don't think Irwin Allen liked westerns because he hired Liberace (not really) as a costuming consultant for the third season, and it meant going back to itchy turtlenecks and colors that eggs in Easter baskets would have "dyed" to have on their shells. The family and I shared tints of mauve, light green, purple, and light yellow with Dr.Smith standing out in his black velour. For the first time, we all upstaged the robot in the costuming department but never in dialogue once the melodious tones of Dick Tufeld were uttered. Liberace got even,though, when he had the opportunity to dress up the robot with a pink boa and another time as a farm girl. These and other get ups gave the robot a myriad of worldly characters to relate to.

The get ups for some of the guest stars were "out of this world." Our show had one woman warrior in a Viking robe wearing a helmet with horns and another dressed in a black sequin outfit with a spiked bowling ball for a headdress. We also had a space pirate, a space cowboy, a space magician, a space devil and space hippies. Who needed to leave earth to enjoy the fantasy world around us? Well, except to experience a multitude of monsters in the dark of night or light of day.

Cyclops was the greatest and most fearsome of all the monsters.

All the others were creative and colorful and sometimes scary, but none of them could hold a boulder over their heads like Cyclops. I have a good story pertaining to one of the monsters. One day, I was standing outside in the area that separated the *Lost in Space* stage from the stage used by *Voyage to the Bottom of the Sea*. A monster in what looked like long strands of red seaweed covering its body came out with a prop man who was carrying a hair dryer. The prop man proceeded to dry the monster off and send him right onto the *Lost in Space* set. Equal opportunity in space!

Maybe I've been overly critical of the costumes on *Lost in Space* because they were perfect as far as our fans were concerned. But what they really loved was the Jupiter 2.

The Spaceship Known as The Jupiter 2

Between the pilot and the first show, I never knew the name of the spaceship changed from Gemini 12 to the Jupiter 2. This was done so that there wouldn't be any confusion with the NASA space program and its Gemini launches. Also, can you believe that I never knew that Don West, in the pilot, was Dr. Donald West. Don't ask me where my head was at when the pilot was being made, but it certainly wasn't focused on the show. I think if I had been told I was going to play a character with the name of Dr. Donald West, I might have thought I was going to be in a comic book adventure with three nephews named Huey, Dewey and Louie. And I wondered, later, what kind of doctor was Donald West? I was to find out that he was a physicist. Spelling it is one thing, but playing the part of such a cerebral character might have disheartened me. As it turned out, being "Crash" West of the Jupiter 2 was just perfect, and "Flash Gordon" didn't sound so bad, after all.

So now, to reminisce about the Jupiter 2. To me, it looked like a spaceship. It was kind of round. It was kind of grey. The design was right out of a light fixture in my hallway. The fixture had a knob so that if you turned it upside down it could go over the bulbs and be easily screwed in and mounted on a ceiling. The design of the inside of the spaceship was a little more complicated. There was something named an astrogator in the middle of the ship that was supposed to replicate an automatic pilot. Its function was to route the ship through space and to navigate it either in interplanetary travel or in interstellar travel. With an astrogator, I thought, what the heck did they need Don West for? Unless of course it got broken which it did once. Because of Dr. Smith's meddling, Don panicked when the ship went defectively berserk. Then Smith and Don both tried to grab the control handle, and we simultaneously pulled it out of the astrogator!

The astrogation unit, I noticed, was smack in the middle of our spaceship which turned out to be very useful. When we were getting pelted by meteors (rolled up balls made out of aluminum foil) and we lost our footing, the astrogation unit gave us a place to hold onto before falling to the other side of the ship. I always made sure I was near Judy so I would have a soft landing place in case I missed grabbing hold of the astrogator.

There was an air lock added to the ship for the first episode, "The Reluctant Stowaway." Earlier in the pilot there was only a large cargo type door that allowed persons to enter and leave the spaceship. Somehow, that cargo door was large enough to accommodate getting the Chariot's parts and the space pod on board. Where were they stored until needed? Well, I guess there was a third deck below on the Jupiter 2. Also, there was a small elevator that supposedly led to the lower deck and was at the back of the ship, not too far from the freezing tubes. They wanted to put in an escalator after the pilot was finished, but the darn robot couldn't handle it without bouncing all the way down and landing on his bubble-head. Not true, but I always wondered if there was a scientific term for the top of the robot or was "bubble-head" the official name for that part? Jonathan Harris made it official with his "bubble-headed booby" nickname for the robot. He also came up with countless names for the robot and the only one I think he missed was "accordion arms."

Anyway, the elevator went from the first floor to a bottom floor. I always perceived the main navigational room as the first floor of the spaceship. That's where the real men hung out. Today they call such a place a "man cave," but in 1965 I called it the "Pilot Penthouse." The women were never to get near the operating panel. After all, they had their kitchen on the bottom deck. John, Will or Don never got in their way of making pies or cakes for Dr. Smith, so no way were they to get in the way of their male counterparts. Wow, I never knew I thought of the show as so sexist. I know it was the sixties, but give me a break! I'm a little apprehensive now about getting into the bedroom assignments, but here goes.

The only bedrooms, or sleeping closets as I called them, were on a level somewhere below the main deck. I never had a tour of the deck that housed the sleeping quarters, but supposedly seven of us, not including the robot, slept there. John and Maureen shared a room, I believe. Judy and I didn't share a room, I believe. Will had his own room, far away from Dr. Smith, and Penny stayed up all night listening to the Beatles and reading Shakespeare so she never slept. Dr. Smith had his own place, close to the kitchen so he could gorge himself while contemplating evil plans. I guess that takes care of every one's beddy-bye time except for the robot. I know it slept standing up, so we could put it anywhere. Maybe in the bathroom, if we had one. If we did, I never used it. I know I wasn't about to wait in line behind six others. How would anyone like to spend three years without using a bathroom? No way, you say! Well, at least there was the hydroponic garden.

What was the hydroponic garden? "Hydro" means "hydroponically grown marijuana" (as defined in Internet <u>slang.com</u>). So, I guess our garden goes a long way to explaining Dr. Smith's behavior. In space, anything goes. The garden was also our food supply. Thank God, because organic vegetables could be very costly. But, money is worthless in space. The nearest supermarket was seven million light years away, and with the price of deutronium at an all time high, the Robinsons gladly took what the good planet gave them. Dr. Smith was overly fussy about the vegetables he ate, and I think that is why the Gods of space turned him into a stalk of celery. I think he looked pretty good, though, as a stalk of celery. A hell of a lot better than the carrot guy. More about that, later.

But now, let's have a brief look at the campsite set up outside the Jupiter 2. Besides having the garden, we had some of our meals at a picnic table because it was easier to film outside. Most of our scenes were played in this area of the Jupiter 2. When we filmed a different scene, we just moved a different styrofoam boulder behind the actors for the new background. It made filming on location very "local." It was as easy as a piece of cake which, it seemed, we were always eating because of birthdays. We even celebrated the robot's birthday on one of our shows. Really! Now, how can we know when a robot was birthed? And how? Can you imagine a mother robot giving birth to our robot? It brings back a line of mine in the script that was never said on camera. It came as I was looking out the view port at an enormous space vehicle that was about to engulf us. It went like this, "It's like nothing I've ever seen before...but twice as big!" I guess that's the kind of a statement you can expect from someone who spent a considerable amount of time in a freezing tube.

The freezing tubes on the Jupiter 2 were the hardware that allowed the crew to make the journey into the far reaches of space. Each member of the family and I had his or her own unbreakable glass enclosure in which to be frozen in time. We were to be in suspended animation for ninety-eight space years or five and one-half earth years. If the suspended animation didn't work for some reason, I would have been 126 years old when we reached our destination.

And I was supposed to colonize the universe? I don't think so. Of course, Judy would have only been 118 years old, so I suppose she could have looked for a younger man, closer to her age, with whom she could share some romantic lunches.

Me? Back on earth, I could care less about romance. It was all about fun! My usual partner for lunch was young William Mumy. Why? Because, Billy was eleven going on twenty-nine, and I was twenty-nine going on eleven. The perfect match. We both liked to have fun, and we both had wild and curious imaginations. Why did Billy's mother, Muriel Mumy, trust her brilliant, talented, angelic son with me? That's a question I have always asked myself. I guess because she honestly liked me and never suspected that I was a prankster. I never suspected that I was a prankster, either. Things just came into my mind for no apparent reason, and I acted on them. I never did anything that could be dangerous or hurt anyone's feelings. It was simply for laughs, and Billy and I got plenty of laughs from our innocent and innocuous pranks.

The pranks can wait, but first our lunches. Often, Billy and I would make our lunches together more than just having a bite to eat. Our favorite times were having picnics in different way off lands. It was our little secret where we were going and how we were getting there. We packed lunches, and with Billy's mom's blessing we would head off in the direction of the cafeteria. Once past there and feeling safe from prying eyes we would case the grounds for a golf cart.

A studio lot encompasses buildings that house departments over a large area for pre and post production such as transportation, wardrobe, props, and sets. Speaking of sets, a funny thing happened when they built a mock up model of the Jupiter 2. After it was built, because of its size, it didn't fit out of the stage doors, although they were very large. They had to cut the spaceship in half in order to move it outside. I think we used the mock-up Jupiter 2 twice during our three years of production.

At any rate, all of those buildings took up a lot of space on the lot, but it was nothing compared to the back lot which was used to recreate locations around the world. Today, filmmakers go to the desired location to shoot their films. But at that time, films were shot on the back lot which was like a giant fantasy Disneyland. You could be in Japan, China, France, England or anyplace that your imagination would take you.

Before Billy and I reached a desired location for our picnic, we would grab one of the golf carts that were left outside for use by studio executives to get from one place to another. Then we'd take a tour of the back lot and decide where we should park our little vehicle and have our lunch for the day. My favorite recollection of one of our fun picnics was when we chose a bombed out city in Germany. There was rubble everywhere, and you could get a sense of what it looked like during wartime. After consuming our sandwiches, we walked quietly among the destruction when we heard some trucks in the near distance. We looked deadpan at each other and Billy said in a soft voice, "Germans?" We quickly ditched the golf cart among the rubble and took off laughing while running back to the main lot.

One day I suggested that we go to France for lunch. Now, Billy costarred with Jimmy Stewart and Bridget Bardot in the movie, *Dear Brigitte.*

So, kiddingly I asked, "Maybe we can visit Bridget Bardot?"

Billy looked at me with his innocent Will Robinson look, and asked,

"Did you see the movie?"

"Yeah, you were real good." I answered mischievously.

"I'll bet you went just to see me," he said with a smile.

"Why else?" I asked with a big grin on my face.

What a career this kid had!

Although those lunches were enjoyable, I think Billy looked forward mostly to our junkets in my blue Fiat when we went to Santa Monica to eat at Chez Jay's restaurant. What a place to bring an eleven year old! It was small and dark with sawdust and peanut shells on the floor. The front door was always open to let the beer smell out, but the food was excellent. We usually had a good sized hamburger with French fries. For drinks, Billy would have a Roy Rogers, and I'd have a Rob Roy. When we were leaving one day, Jay Fiondella, the owner of this bar where big time Hollywood patrons wined and dined, gave us a shopping bag full of peanuts to bring back to the studio and share with the cast and crew. Immediately, my mind raced at the thought of sharing our peanuts.

The peanut story is *Lost in Space* folklore because of the number of times I have told it, but one more time won't hurt. There are two versions to this tale. Billy's and mine. I like mine, so that is the one I want to share with you.

After reaching the stage we were shooting on, I whispered to Billy to follow me. We went to the back of the stage and climbed up a wooden stairway that led to a platform that led to another stairway that led to another platform and so forth until we were high above the stage where the actors were performing. Gigantic klieg lights were below Billy and me, obscuring anyone's view of where we were. A scene between Dr. Smith and the robot was being rehearsed. I placed the big bag of unshelled peanuts on the platform between us and asked Billy to hand me a peanut as I scoped the scene below. He did so, and I whispered, "Billy, I'll show you what a good shot I was when I played basketball in high school!" I measured my aim and made a one-handed push shot with the peanut that landed on the bubble of the robot. PING !! I grinned with pleasure and picked up the bag of peanuts. "Let's go before we get caught," I said in a low voice. "No, wait," an enthused Billy spurted out as he grabbed the bag of peanuts from me and triumphantly sprayed them from above with peanuts landing on all the unsuspecting victims below. Everyone looked to the rafters to see where the peanuts, raining on them, came from. At the time I thought, "They'll never know!" Now, Billy's version has me up in the rafters alone, but I think that's what he wants to believe for fear of us coming so close to having been caught.

But, we never did get caught for our pranks. We came close the time we locked Bob May in the robot outfit, but I never sweated it because I had the perfect shield for not getting in trouble. Who would believe I was capable of leading young William Mumy astray? No one! We were a team and too clever, like the heroes in the comic Billy made about the two of us, *Captain Panther and The Fox*. He was the perfect accomplice. But then, what couldn't he do? Billy could act, play the guitar beautifully and write his own songs besides creating characters for comics he so cleverly drew. All that and being a good friend to everyone on the set made him stand out as a very special person which he remains to this day.

The John and Don Show

Professor Robinson and I had quite a relationship. We had our moments of disagreement, but we liked and trusted each other. Without that friendship the space ship that we traveled in would never have made it to anywhere with all the problems we faced. We faced a quicksand pit. We faced being locked in an abandoned space vehicle. We faced the danger of a poisonous desert. How did we get in and out of these and other problems?

Take the time we were caught in a cave and a one eyed giant wanted to crush us by thrusting an uprooted tree into the cave. How did that come about?

Well, we were on one of our walks in a mountainous area when we came across a giant footprint. I wanted to turn around and go back to the spaceship, but John's curiosity got the better of him and he insisted on proceeding. We followed giant footprint after giant footprint until, you guessed it, we came upon a real live giant! He was enormous and we didn't want any part of him, so we ran into a nearby cave. I guess we hoped we could stay there safely until he decided to go back to his giant wife. But he was persistent and kept poking that tree at us which was getting closer and closer. I was getting pretty angry at this point and decided to do something clever. Having been an Eagle Scout, I had my trusty pouch with me that contained a flare and kitchen matches. I always wanted to give someone a hotfoot, and now I had my chance. Without telling John my plan, I lit the match and tossed the flare outside the cave in the direction of the giant's foot. The fearsome hulk stepped on it like it was a firefly without giving me the satisfaction of even a whimper. What it did do, though, was make the giant angrier than I was, and he let out a roar that scared the living, you know what, out of both of us. John gave me a scowl that was nearly as scary. We were doomed. I was sure of it. What could save us?

And then I remembered young Will Robinson! There was daylight at the end of the cave after all. I saw the flash of a laser beam. I heard the thud of a fallen giant that shook my fur-lined hoody right off of my head. We then heard the warm sound of "Dad."

We both hurried outside to hear Will say with some bravado, "Dad, I shot the Giant!" I got out of there fast so I wouldn't have to listen to John telling Will that he disobeyed orders and should never have left the space ship. "Oh, by the way, thanks for saving our lives, but don't you ever do it again!" If I had stayed, I would have said to Will, "Thanks, kid. That was a nice shot, even better than the one David used to take out Goliath." But I never got the chance.

Then there was the quicksand story. By definition, quicksand is a pit filled with loose wet sand into which objects get sucked down. Well, I didn't want to be one of the objects that gets sucked down so when John stupidly got caught in the quagmire, I had to think quickly. I had a rope with me. I tried to make a lasso but was never taught how to do that in my Eagle Scout training book, so I just threw the line out to my fast sinking friend. He grabbed it and yanked. In fact, he yanked the rope so hard that I found myself next to him in the quicksand. Now, we were both waist deep. As we sunk deeper and deeper, I kept waiting for young Will Robinson to show up again. No such luck. But I hoped that maybe, if he saw us on the radio telescope like he did when he saved us from the giant, he might come to where we were and save us again. We were sinking fast and no Will.

I got angry at the thought of him, cosy in the spaceship, playing chess with the robot. And, I thought, as the quicksand reached my chest area, why wasn't the robot ever with John and Don on our dangerous episodes? You never heard, "Danger, danger Don West!" did you? No! Because all he ever cared about was Will Robinson. I thought we were doomed. But, at least our arms were still free and we both had a good hold on the rope which John managed to tie to a low hanging branch. With all the strength he had, and using me as a plank of wood, he clawed his way out of the quicksand. Then he casually brushed off his tight fitting pants and began combing his hair. "Hey, what about me?" I yelled as I spit out a mouthful of sand. "Yeah, what about you?" he asked. "Do you promise always to be faithful to my daughter, Judy, when you get married?" The sand was now getting in my ear and there is nothing worse than sand in your ear. I had no choice but to raise my sinking hand in surrender.

That is how I remember and fantasize about the quicksand episode, but how it went down was really like this: John and Don and Smith were out prospecting when some plants pulled John and Don into quicksand.

Smith ran back to the space ship and told Will who came back with a rope. How dull! I prefer my version of the adventure, but you decide.

Another adventure centered around finding an abandoned space vehicle. It wasn't very big. It looked like a one manned space vehicle of some kind. Vines and weeds had entangled it, so it obviously had been there for some time. We climbed the short ladder stairs and entered. No one was home, and it was very musty and dark. As we looked at a hammock with the name Captain Alonzo P. Tucker printed on it, the heavy door of the vehicle closed shut. John immediately reached for a latch or lever to open it. Nothing! We were encased in a vault with no way to escape. No windows, no opening, no nothing. I felt dread. I looked at my partner, John. He looked at me. Soon, there would be no oxygen to keep us alive. What to do? I looked at John again. He looked at me again. Here we were, two heroes about to save the entire universe by colonization, and we had locked ourselves in some kind of archaic space vehicle. We looked around for a marker that would unlock the door. There was a panel of buttons, but which one would open it?

Even though I flew the Jupiter by pushing buttons, I was skeptical about doing the same on a space ship I knew nothing about. We almost took off when I pressed the first button. The spaceship shook like a cranked up Tin Lizzie. The second button did nothing, but a switch below it finally opened the door. We got out of there, greatly relieved, but curious about who this Tucker guy was.

The next escapade was quick and of little consequence. Our environmental robot suspected that there was poisonous gas in the desert not too far from our spaceship. Of course, John and I decided to make the area safe for the family. John made a sign attached to a stake that read, **DANGER** - POISONOUS GAS - **KEEP AWAY** - Order of **John Robinson**. As we trekked out to this remote section of the desert, I asked John, "Why are we always doing these menial tasks?" He shot back, "Because we are the men-ials."

We had taken Smith and Will along with us to help set up the drilling equipment for fuel not far from the poisonous gas location. I stayed back with Will and Smith as John ventured into the dangerous area of the desert to put up his warning sign. He proved the warning to be true when he pounded the stake into the ground letting the poisonous gas escape. The result knocked him out flatter than a pancake! When some time had passed, Will went to check on him. Finding his dad unconscious, he hurried back to the drill site for help. I dragged his limp six-foot four, one hundred and ninety pound body to safety. It was the hardest physical work I did in my three years on *Lost in Space.*

The Cast of *Lost in Space*

Everyone always asked what it was it like working with the cast from *Lost in Space*. There are two responses needed to that question. There were the "real"(actual) people I worked with as Mark and the "reel" (on film) people I worked with as Don. As Mark, I was fortunate to be with the best of the best. I can't be flip when it comes to discussing the "real" cast from the show. When I get to the "reel" cast, I can be a little irreverent. So let's get to know the relationships from Mark and Don's perspective.

First up, the Robinson family. John Robinson was portrayed by Guy Williams. After fifty years, a lot of people get us mixed up. After all, we both were tall, dark and handsome. Well, one of us was, and I am glad to defer to "Guido," the nickname June Lockhart loved to call him. Hard core devotees of the show would not get us mixed up, but casual viewers might. What I get is, "Oh, yeah, you were the pilot, or you were the blonde's boyfriend, or you were the one who hated Dr. Smith. That's fine with me because the fans give me credit, after all these years, for existing.

Well, Guy existed. Boy, did he exist! As I said, he was tall, dark and handsome as the saying went in the golden days of Hollywood. He was the type that defined the Hollywood star. Except for timing (the end of the studio star system), Guy would have been a movie star instead of a television star. Zorro made him the TV star for which he will always be remembered. I found, in real life, that Guy had the flair and romantic aspect of the character he so wonderfully portrayed. He loved fine red wines, fine respectable women and fine classical music. Me? Give me a cold beer, a pretty blonde and a Rock&Roll song, any day. Different from one another? You bet! But a bond of friendship and trust between us was something you could also bet on. He drove a red Maserati and I drove a blue Fiat, but when we took either one to the race track we had a great time. Guy loved numbers. He made money by being a terrific handicapper of horses and a whiz in the stock market. Me? Once again, I would end up losing money at the track and in the stock market. C'est la vie!

As the professor and the pilot, we had a more restrained relationship. As I related in the *John and Don* section of this book, together we never did anything right. By himself, John Robinson or sometimes his alter ego usually accomplished his goal. I never did. I crashed the Jupiter 2 on a number of occasions. I lost every fight I engaged in. I fell off the Chariot trying to fix the solar panel apparatus with my trusty solar wrench. When I finally kissed Judy, it was on the hand. Even my negative alter ego couldn't keep John Robinson from escaping in the "Anti- Matter Man" episode. So, needless to say, the good professor didn't trust me or think I would be a suitable husband for his beautiful daughter, Judy. Once again, C'est la vie.

I don't think Maureen Robinson particularly cared for me as a suitor for her daughter, either. Like there was a choice? The Space Cowboy? The Space Pirate? The Space Magician? Maybe Mr. Nobody would be a better suitor than me. Maybe, but Penny already had her eyes set on him. There was also Dr. Smith and the robot, but nobody wanted to break up that twosome. Maureen just didn't think I was good enough for "The girl of my dreams," her musical comedy actress of a daughter. I guess I can't blame her, though. I was cocky, unreliable, and kind of a gadfly. Besides, I was always taking her husband on some useless trip to the weather station or drilling site so he never did the chores around the spaceship like other husbands did. No kidding! Did you ever see John Robinson sweep the deck or clean the viewing window on the Jupiter 2. No. You never did. You know why? Because he was off with me on one of those useless forays or showing off his manliness by fighting some stupid aliens. As if it were my fault that he loved showing off his excellent marksmanship or his acrobatic use of a sword! There was no way that I had anything to do with the escapades he got himself into. But, who was going to tell Maureen that? I really believe that she thought I was a bad influence on her husband. She was attracted to his sensitive, compassionate side, and I was attracted, in a lionhearted way, to his macho, warrior side. Actually, Maureen and I hardly ever talked to each other except for the time she told me not to drive off in the Chariot until John got back from looking for Penny. That was our "reel" relationship.

As for our "real" personal relationship, June and I communicated beautifully. She was a "hoot" as she so often referred to me. What a lovely lady. Pure class when it came to treating the cast and crew in her elegant style. I enjoyed the company of this exquisite lady both at her home in Brentwood and in her dressing room trailer on the lot at 20th Century Fox Studio. She was fun, fun, fun and invited everyone to her party. She could create the moment, or she could take a daffy occurrence and turn it into a memorable escapade. I can think of two incidences that perfectly demonstrate her delightful sense of humor and her gentle spirit. The first involved Jonathan and has made the rounds at panel discussions on the show. During a convention, June disguised herself as a homeless bag lady and approached Jonathan's table. She searched laboriously for the picture she wanted him to sign, and after she found it and it was signed, June put out her hand to shake Jonathan's. Being polite, he shook her hand not knowing that June had put some garlic spread on her palm. Jonathan, smelling the oily ooze, was gracious but mortified as he bid her farewell. The look on his face was pure Dr. Smith when June removed her oversized bonnet and revealed herself. It was all good fun though, and that is how Jonathan responded to the prank.

The second incident is more tomfoolery than a prank. It includes me and is less well known, except as a conversation piece when June and I would share this amusing story. It was linked to a fan letter I received from Grinnell, Iowa. I had badly injured my foot in an episode where John and I (another John and Don escapade) were in a remote desert area (is there any other kind?) and a large boulder fell on my foot, pinning it against another rock. I laid there in great agony, moaning, in the best Don West style I could muster as John attempted to release my foot from the pressure of the rocks. Well, the guy who wrote the letter had fallen in love with my foot. He wanted to know all the measurements so he could make a plaster cast of my foot. He also desired any unused audio tracks of the incident so he could enjoy the excruciating pain that I was experiencing. I couldn't wait to show the letter to June. Boy oh boy, did she know how to reply to that letter. Her letter contained the following puns, "I'm glad you admire my heroic *feats*," "I am kind of a *footloose* and carefree guy," "Actually, I am about six *feet* tall," and "*Football* is my favorite sport" among many more. I signed it, and we sent it off to the return address. June discovered later that Grinnell housed the largest mental institution in Iowa. She also found out, to our relief, that the young man's address was not the same as the mental institution's address.

June had a myriad of interests and was also known as the Rock and Roll Goddess. And for good reason. Once she hosted "The Hour Glass," at her home, who later became known as "The Allman Brothers." They were also guests of June's on the set. Photos were taken of the group with the cast members. Billy and Angela were very excited about this visit. I could have cared less because I didn't know who the heck they were. Anyway, whether discussing politics, playing Scrabble, enjoying music, or engaging in casual conversation, Mrs. Robinson's dressing room was always accessible and she was always hospitable. She was (and still is) the darling of NASA. It is a joy to hear her recount her relations with the organization that is responsible for our space program. And she loved her antique fire engine that she occasionally drove to work at the 20th Century Fox Studio. Maybe the fire engine was old, but June was always young in her attitude toward life. She lived it to the fullest during our three years on *Lost in Space.* She was the real thing, but the "reel" thing now for our consideration is Maureen's eldest daughter, Judy.

Maureen was reasonably protective of this beautiful, talented young woman. After all, she won a beauty contest against the ugliest participants in space. Of course, this was Smith's doing. I advised against Judy getting involved in the competition. But, because I half-heartedly gave her the impression that she might not win, she signed Smith's silly contract. You just can't joke around about a woman's beauty. No, sir! Not on earth and not in space. Judy was a true beauty, a beauty who even plants wanted to kidnap as one of their own. Even the Devil himself was wantonly and lustfully desirous of our blonde haired Barbie Doll look alike. But, once again, to prove my worth as a suitable suitor, I came to the rescue, only to be knocked out by a frantic Judy trying to escape the evil clutches of the Devil. She used a lyre to lay me out. Who says it has to be beauty or brawn?

The "real" Judy, Marta Kristen was, however, as gentle in spirit as she was beautiful. As a young child, she was adopted by a wonderful couple in Michigan. She found her way to Hollywood with their blessing and went on to have a successful career.

During our three years together on the show, Marta and I had a very cordial relationship. I must admit I had a crush on Marta, but it wasn't a crush that would destroy our friendship. I mean how could any male worth his salt be in close proximity for three years to a gorgeous young female and not have a tiny crush. I was that male. She was that female. That was our story. I hate to disappoint the fans who like a little romantic fantasy when it comes to Marta and me, but we were true to ourselves and our mates. I will say this about her; she stood up for her rights and became slightly competitive when it was apparent that she wasn't getting the screen time she deserved. I was fine with my role because I had meaningful scenes with Guy and Smith that were at least satisfying. But not so when it came to Marta. She didn't have a lot to do when the show first came on the air. I used to do a bit, at the early conventions, when I would mimic Marta coming out of the Jupiter 2, onto the platform, looking about and loudly whispering, "Will"? Then when she complained to Irwin that she needed more to do, he promised her she would have it in the next show. So, as I would recall it to the convention audience, on the next show, Marta came out of the Jupiter 2 and she looked to the left and loudly whispered, "Will"? Then she looked to the right and loudly whispered "Penny"? Marta has a wonderful sense of humor as evidenced by her laughter when I performed this bit while she shared the stage with me.

Judy's sister was portrayed by Angela Cartwright. She had a smile that radiated innocence to everyone around her. Quiet? I guess so, but inside that creative, bright mind was a thirst for learning. Photography and music were her main interests. In fact, she had the privilege of attending a soiree where she met and talked with the Beatles. That meeting is a very special memory for Angela. Having an American/ British dual citizenship made her twice the well mannered young lady so many fans adored. Her mother, an unassuming, gracious woman, was on the stage with her at all times. She was the protecter of both Angela and Angela's character, Penny, who never had a hint of anything but delight emanating from her angelic face. True to character, even when her pet monkey, Debbie, bit her on the finger, she didn't make a big deal of it. It was a pleasure to have her on the show.

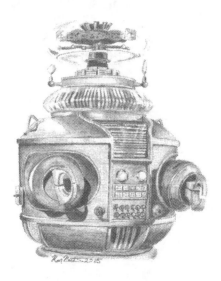

Before moving on to the last family member, Will Robinson, I'd like to take a detour as Crash West would to talk about the robot and Dr. Smith. First, let's reminisce about the robot from Don West's perspective. He was a foil to Dr. Smith. Without the robot, Smith wouldn't have lasted as a character on the show. Whether as a villain early on, or as a campy personality later, Smith and the robot were meant to be together. The robot was supposed to be the guardian of the Robinson family, but Dr. Smith ("Colonel" then) programmed him to destroy the very people he was created to protect. I always thought he was goofy looking and clumsy. He did fall over once going up the ramp to the spaceship when someone stepped on the pulley wire that was used to transport him. It wasn't me, honest! When he fell back on the ramp, the robot costume separated into three distinct parts. When I looked, I saw the bubble, the body, and the legs separated in a way only a magician could make happen because Bob May was still inside the encasement. Can you believe that? Or for that matter, the robot's accomplishments?

The robot could do everything. He sang. He played the guitar. He played chess. He baked pies. He painted portraits. He danced with natives to their music. He flew the pod. He even impersonated a woman when draped with a pink boa around his round body. Most importantly, though, he destroyed enemies of the Robinsons, read minds and was a loyal valet to Dr. Smith. To tell you the truth, I was jealous of all of his achievements. I think the robot and I could have been good friends if we ever had the opportunity to get to know one another. We both had a pretty good sense of humor, but the robot's laugh, guffaw really, irritated the hell out of me. We both had cute smiles, and we both had an an eye for the opposite sex. Although he didn't have an eye, he had something that drew him to female mechanical robots. And when he wasn't flirting with a shapely piece of metal, he was making nice with Smith back at the ship's campsite. That, however, also irritated me because I was hard at work at the drilling site or at the weather station with John. I mean how would he like it if I stayed back flirting with Judy while he was sent to dig ditches for security reasons? But then again, a robot is only a robot, unless you give it a personality.

That brings us to Bob May who gave the robot its persona. My feelings toward Bob May were conflicted because he was an enigma. On one hand, he worked very hard on the set. On the other hand, his attitude of self-importance was irritating not only to me and others in the show but especially to Jonathan Harris. I always felt humility was what we should respect in others, but humility was not a word in Bob's vocabulary. Unlike the robot, who did everything, Bob professed to have done just about everything on celluloid, but outside of *Lost in Space* how much impact did he really have in the world of show business? It is true that he was raised in an environment that centered around vaudeville. His grandfather was one-half of the Olsen and Johnson comedy team, and he wasn't shy about letting everyone know it. He was proud of his lineage, and as he liked to tell it, he was born in a trunk. Above anything else, he was determined to use his robot notoriety to get back to those glory days.

At one point, after *Lost in Space*, Bob put together a vaudeville act featuring the one and only Bob May so he could publicize the act as produced, directed and starring Bob May. With a sum of money lent by an unsuspecting fan and friend, he travelled across the country by train to realize his fantasy. He had planned to stop at certain towns on the way to Florida. He had the stunt robot with him and a team of men who would put Bob in the costume, help him out of it, and make the bubble-headed booby work. He made it to Florida, his final destination, but he ran out of money and stranded the workers with their robot in alligator land. What happened? As told to me by someone on this journey across America, Bob booked one night performances in different towns. To promote these performances he placed flyers the size of postcards in the windows of the train that was traveling at sixty miles an hour. I can't imagine what could have gone wrong with that ingenious way of advertising his show.

At one performance, Bob got furious when the curtain stayed down before his second curtain call. Only three people were in the audience! That's not exactly a packed house, and this is not a made up story. I was told it by one of the robot prop workers who wasn't happy about the time he spent and the money he was owed. The masked robot struck again!

Why masked? As most of you know, Bob May had black grease put around his eyes to resemble the black eyed mask of a raccoon. This was done so the audience couldn't detect flesh which would make them aware that there was a human being inside the costume. He also wore a black shirt, black slacks and black shoes. Now picture this! Dressed like that, Bob went to the bank one day to make a deposit during lunch break. When he returned to the makeup room, he said to those who would listen, "You wouldn't believe this but when I was standing in the teller's line everyone was looking at me. They must have recognized me as the robot from *Lost in Space.*" "Sure, Bob," I laughed. "I'll bet that black mask and black clothes really gave you away!"

Bob didn't get the sarcastic comments I threw his way. I suppose I was taking advantage of his naïveté, but went ahead and did it anyway. What made it worse was that he seemed to like me, and I kept wishing that he didn't. It conjured up guilt feelings in my, otherwise, untroubled mind. Jonathan was far more sarcastic with his quick wit, but it all went right over the bubble. Jonathan, bless him, never felt a bit of remorse and didn't really care what Bob might think or care what he might say. Sometimes, there were no words to explain how I felt about what Bob would say. At times, he just outdid himself. That was the case on a particular day in England.

Bob and I with others, including Connie Stevens and Lana wood, were making an appearance in

London. We were in a bus seated close to one another, leaving the hotel on our way to the appearance site, when Bob started in on his army days. He mentioned he was stationed down south on an army base where he organized a football team and broke his leg while playing. He went on to say that he received the Purple Heart because of the injury. We were all dumbstruck (appropriate when Bob was speaking), but said nothing. Finally, I questioned him by stating that Purple Hearts are only awarded to a soldier when wounded in combat. He brushed it off and went on to other subjects concerning celebrities like Jerry Lewis (who he said was a close friend) and Elvis Presley (who he said dated his wife.) His questionable stories came at a fast clip and made us wonder about the truth of his experiences. No one though except me, questioned him to his face, but all eyes went skyward when he attempted to make himself a renowned Hollywood star.

There was the time, for instance, when June, Marta and I were guests on a talk show in Detroit. The show was called "Kelly and Company." Bob was also a guest. The three of us took a car to the studio, but Bob showed up in a limo with three body guards. He told the audience that he needed them because he owned a semi-professional football team. He placed them in the audience so they could direct questions to Bob during the telecast. At one point, off air, Bob was explaining to Kelly that when he checks into a hotel, because of his star power, he does so under an assumed name that no one has ever heard. I interrupted him at this point, and told Kelly that I did the same thing. I always checked in under the name of BOB MAY.

This went on and on whenever Bob and I were together. I'm told the same things happened with other cast members. There was the time he was on a personal appearance tour in Australia. He was with Dick Tufeld, the voice of the robot, who was a very talented and humble man. As the story goes, Bob embarrassed Dick when he accused the Aborigine natives, when introduced to them, of being culturally uninformed for not knowing that he was the robot from *Lost in Space*. Well, I know how badly Bob must have felt. When I toured Australia, I also took my six year old son to see the Aborigine natives perform their tribal dance. Do you believe they didn't recognize my son as being the son of the guy who played Don West on *Lost in Space*! Indeed! How dare they not know!!

Okay, I'm telling these stories about Bob May with a personal bias but for a reason. I could take his exaggerations and his cocky, "Do you know who I am?" attitude, but the time he broke the heart of a friend of the cast of *Lost in Space* I knew our working relationship could never be restored.

The cast was doing a convention in New Jersey called Chiller Theater. It's a big venue that attracts some forty-thousand people. We were in a tented area, outside of the hotel, with lines of fans waiting to get autographs. Among those waiting was a young lady and her husband who are die-hard fans of our show. Their house is practically a shrine to *Lost in Space* with a complete room of memorabilia and a wall of autographed pictures. Everything they have was purchased from the cast over a number of years. We all got to know this couple with a deep appreciation for their love of the show. They came especially to see us, and it cost them a pretty penny to do so. But to them, it was well worth it because we spent time chatting with them, and once in awhile I would give them extra autographed pictures or a memento. On this particular Saturday, the couple moved down the cast's line of tables and reached Bob May. The young lady was buying pictures from him like she had done, so often, in the past. I was seated next to Bob, so I couldn't help but notice how upset she was when she left his table.

I got up and followed her outside. She was sobbing. Her husband was trying to console her, and I could see she was attempting to hide her tears from me. We went to a more secluded area, and she related what had happened at Bob's table. She told me that she had bought some items and pictures when she noticed a thick pamphlet on his table. She thumbed through it and thought it was an interesting piece about *Lost in Space*. It was made up of press clippings put out by the Sci-Fi Channel, announcing an up coming television marathon of *Lost in Space*. No pictures. Just copies of the same press releases that appeared in different newspapers. She asked Bob to sign it, thinking it couldn't cost too much. That is where our friend made a mistake. He charged her $500 for his autograph on this piece of nothing. I sensed that her hurt was a personal feeling of deception from a *Lost in Space* friend.

I came back inside the tent, fuming. There was a line of people waiting to get my signature because I had been gone for so long, but I composed myself so I could present a happy face to our loyal fans. When the day ended, Bob scooted away, and I didn't have a chance to confront him about the unfair advantage he took of a loyal fan. It was months later at a Ray Courts show at the Beverly Garland Hotel in Burbank, California that I finally had the opportunity to let him have it the way Don West would have done. Angrily, I asked him how he could do this to such a good friend of the actors in *Lost in Space*. I came close to hammering him but held myself back as a restrained Don West would have done. I never spoke to him again in a friendly manner.

Despite that incident, I have to admit that Bob was a loving husband and a wonderful father. That's more important than a tin suit, but something happened to him once he got into that outfit. He forgot who he was. And he was in that outfit a lot! Bob spent more hours in that hot robot costume than he did in his own home. He was either in robot gear or in his dressing room trailer, which he painted silver on the inside to match the color of the robot. He became obsessed with the mechanical marvel. Now, I've said kiddingly at conventions (before he died) that he became so obsessed with the robot that if one day he had twin boys he would name them Ro and Bot. Okay, he wouldn't have done that, but it says a lot about his fascination with his metallic self. This alter ego of Bob's had many, many names created by the talented Jonathan Harris.

Jonathan, as we all know, was the consummate professional. He did, indeed, as he liked to put it, create all the names he flippantly called his companion and adversary. I think my favorite moniker was "animated hunk of machinery." He worked tirelessly on his scripts and fine tuned his lines to fit his character. He was always in the make-up chair when called and loved to needle Bob Marks, the make-up artist, whom he called the plumber. On the set, he was aware of everything that was going on. He knew camera angles, proper lighting, scene coverage (the director's prerogative), and, most importantly, how his character would react to any situation. (That reminds me of a quote by the fine actress, Joanne Woodward, "Acting is reacting.") He had his tricks, but they were all above board. I noticed when we worked together that he always made sure the camera shot would end on him. If, in the scene, I had the last line Jonathan would add an "Indeed!" or whatever was needed to have his close up end the dialogue. It worked and it was good for the scene.

In between scenes, actors either went to their dressing rooms or stayed on the set to chat or rehearse lines with each other. During a scene, while the lighting was being prepared for the next shot, the actors usually sat in their canvassed back chairs that had been designated for them to relax in. It was the only opportunity that the regular cast members got to converse with the guest stars or steal a smoke. (Yes, it was the sixties and I smoked as Marta did and Guy would sneak a cigar once in a while.) Jonathan, however, rarely sat on the set between scenes. He was much too busy studying lines and reworking the dialogue to suit his character. Dr. Smith didn't just happen. He was created in the mind of a very dedicated actor. Jonathan knew what he wanted, and he knew how to get it. Hard work! Today, I consider him the Larry Bird of *Lost in Space*. Like Larry, his work ethic was impeccable, and he made the actors he was performing with act better because of his perfectionist attitude. To me, Larry Bird was the hardest working and greatest basketball player of his time. If I mentioned Larry Bird to Jonathan, he would have probably raised an eyebrow and asked, "Any relation to Lady Bird?"

While we loved to banter, I felt I could always learn something from Jonathan. The only interest that I could possibly educate him about was sports, and he wasn't into sports. But, he, himself was always a good sport. He was fun to josh with because of his quick wit and unapologetic attitude. We shared more than a few drinks together during dinners at various conventions. There would be others sharing this time, and they were treated to some raucous humor by both Jonathan and me. I must say that neither of us were politically correct, and some four letter words were thrown around with the precision of Tom Brady passes. If I said that to my good friend, Jonathan, he would come back with, "What's a Tom Brady? My goodness, is that a disguised Mickey Finn?" He had a remarkable sense of humor, and I enjoyed his wit tremendously. But, only at work or conventions. You see, friendships were not usually extended past the workplace, unless the parties had a shared passion for something. Jonathan loved the opera. I couldn't share this passion that he had so meticulously cultivated. I thought Figaro was the bodybuilder who played the Incredible Hulk.

Jonathan was a homebody. I was everybody's home buddy. I never met his wife while he was alive or his son, for that matter, although I have heard nothing but nice things about the two of them. Jonathan was a very private man with a deep and analytical mind. I've been pretty public about my life and a way of thinking that couldn't find its way out of the shallow end of a swimming pool. But, while having our cocktails, Jonathan became pretty public, and my mind started searching in the deep end of the pool for the meaning of life! We never felt closer than when we shared those times over a drink or two.

On screen, Don West was more ambiguous about Dr. Smith. He was the worst kind of human being. Think of all the terrible things he did on *Lost in Space!* He almost got us killed on numerous occasions. He was a liar and a thief and turned some alien friends against the Robinson family. These aliens (although, I guess, *we* were the aliens) might have been able to help us get back to our mission in space. But Dr. Smith was so greedy he continuously screwed everything up. He lusted for anything of value that he could horde and take back to Earth with him and stole from the space creatures as well. That really angered me because he kept putting our lives in danger over mere "stuff." I would have made sure, if we ever got back, that he would pay for sabotaging our mission. Prison, maybe? I also would have loved to clock him, just once.

I never did get to clock Smith, though, because my opportunities were always thwarted by the niceness, compassion and forgiveness of the Robinson clan. That's what I never got! Whenever he was close to being banished from our camp, Maureen was gooey with sympathy. Judy showed nothing but pity. John was far too lenient. Will was ready to cry, and Penny was too busy listening to the Beatles to care. On the other hand, I wanted to be rid of him and felt I should have dumped him in outer space long ago. His eventual banishment wasn't for his worse offense, but it really irked me. Using our severely limited water supply to shower his boney body was incomprehensible, even for the selfish Dr. Smith. To make it worse, the robot was his accomplice. The bucket of bolts should also have been banished!

While Dr. Smith is the yang of my recollections about *Lost in Space*, Will Robinson is the yin, and that is why I saved him for last. The Don West/Will Robinson relationship was good, but not as good as the Mark Goddard/Billy Mumy camaraderie. As I mentioned earlier, Billy and I loved to have escapades off the set, but our friendship was even more meaningful to me. He always had a smile to give me and with that smile came respect. Age difference put aside, we communicated on an equal level. It was like we knew what each other was thinking. His musical talent was evolving daily and, unfortunately, my musical vibes were stuck in the fifties. But, it didn't get in the way of our sharing our appreciation for each other's musical taste. I remember giving him the LP record of *"The Roar of the Greasepaint"* which was on Broadway at the time. He loved it and in return went on to play all the music of The Kingston Trio for me. We were good to each other and were also kind and loving to each other's families. His mother, Muriel, was like a big sister to me. And whenever my four year old daughter visited the set, she had Billy's full attention for the short time she was there. Even with a heavy work schedule and school, he always treated my wife, Marcia, and my daughter, Missy, with a warm greeting. Whether we were riding in my blue Fiat or opening peanuts at Chez Jay's restaurant, we were buddies all the way. But, we were not as chummy on the show.

Don West was a hothead, and Will Robinson was the coolest kid this side of Alpha Centauri. I was jealous that I would never have a son like Will Robinson. Maybe later, but our being lost in space was not an encouraging sign for fatherhood. I might have gotten to kiss Judy on the cheek after a ten year engagement process, but I wouldn't have bet on it. And by that time, her little brother would have become a big brother who was protecting her, so a little necking in the chariot would have definitely been out. Well, not definitely. Will had a romantic side, and when he grabbed hold of his guitar, look out ladies. But, where were the ladies? The only females we came into contact with were either green (perfect for Kermit the frog) or pretty women with strong feminist attitudes that would have wilted even Will's romantic fantasies. As I've said, he was only eleven when I crashed landed on our first planet, but he was going on thirty. He really had it together. One time, he looked at me in such an adult way that you could practically read his mind as if he were thinking, "Where did this jerk get his license, at Sears and Roebuck?" But mostly, he treated me like an invited house guest who was glad that the guest stayed longer than expected. Will and Don West got along, yet, something was missing in our relationship.

I had no family and could never really be part of Will's family. I never had any moments of fatherly understanding like John had with Will or musical moments like he had with Judy (maybe because I couldn't carry a tune or play an instrument). And more importantly, while Will was Mr. Reliable, I was "Crash" West.

Now, let's find out how I ended up with the moniker "Crash West" by looking at some of the more memorable episodes of *Lost in Space*, starting with "the Reluctant Stowaway" and ending with

"The Great Vegetable Rebellion." In addition to giving the storyline for each episode in regular print, I've included my own thoughts in **bold** print and created imaginary thoughts and dialogue for Don West which have been *italicized.*

Like the unforgettable Bette Davis said in a movie, "buckle up, boys and girls, it's going to be a bumpy ride." Could you expect anything less with Don "Crash" West piloting this baby?

The Episodes

"The Reluctant Stowaway"

ALL EPISODE ILLUSTRATIONS BY PERRY CORVESE 2016

Our initial episode is "The Reluctant Stowaway" So, what is this show all about? This unique family will be the first family in space, the first to reach beyond the outer limits, and the first to colonize the universe. The trip will take ninety-eight earth years, and the crew will be in suspended animation for that time. *Hey, that sounds pretty cool. But what the hell is suspended animation? Ninety-eight years? That's a long time to go without any hoochie coochie, not to mention* *spaghetti and meatballs.* **Don, suspended animation means the crew will be frozen for five and one-half years in space, which is equal to ninety-eight earth years.** *I get it, but what's this about colonizing the entire universe? Wait a minute! Did Alpha Control commit to this? Is that what they're expecting? Who is supposed to do this? John Robinson isn't going to have any more children and his son, Will, didn't take a girlfriend along so who the heck does that leave? Me! I should have pursued getting to know the oldest daughter better. She's real pretty and I think we would have beautiful children, but have I been set up? I haven't been with a woman for a while, and I could use some good old fashioned companionship but, like they say, there are a lot of fish in the ocean. Except, to me, it looks like I'm in a rowboat on the Dead Sea with a family who has the only age appropriate fish in sight. Ninety-eighty earth years?*

After the ship goes off course because of the added weight of a covert foreign agent named Colonel Smith, the Jupiter 2 is hit by a slew of meteors. **What a waste of tinfoil. Couldn't Irwin Allen afford any real meteors?** While in suspended animation, Don is motionless. *I'm having this fantastic dream about my relationship with Judy, but I keep hearing these smashing sounds. I must be having a nightmare in this freezing tube, or the ship is in trouble and I can't move a muscle to do anything about it.* Smith opens the freezing tube door and Major West falls out. *What the heck is going on? I feel like a frozen pork chop that was just taken out of the freezer. I'd like to finish my dream about Judy, but now*

she's slapping my face and I haven't even tried to kiss her.
Smith is kneeling by Don's head and slapping him in
the face to awaken him. Don wakes up and looks at
Smith, face to face, in an upside down position. *How
did this stranger get in my dream? Now, I know this is a
nightmare. This isn't the face of an angel; it's the face of
the devil.* After coming to his senses, Don evaluates
the situation. Smith has, meanwhile, been tinkering
with the robot who goes berserk and smashes the
astrogator. Don fights the robot while trying to
get its power pack. **Don doesn't exactly float like
a butterfly and sting like a bee when fighting a
machine.** *How do I fight this fat tin-can? I'll kick it in
the groin, but where the heck is its groin? Grab the power
pack! This doodad is too fast for me. Duck and grab. Good!
I've got it.*

Once the fight is over, the rest of the family becomes
conscious. No one is sure what to do, and Don shuts
off the gravity. **Why would he do that? I guess he
thinks the kids would be better off floating around
and being out of the way while he tries to pilot the
ship. Now, the Robinsons are really on their way
to being lost in space.** John shows up. *"Where have
you been? I'm glad you decided to join me, John. I just
fought the robot and kicked his rubberized ass!"* It's been
decided that John has to take a walk in space to fix a
broken scanner. John puts on his space walking gear
and is ready to make the repair. Tension fills the air
inside the Jupiter as they watch John make his way
to the scanner. But, there is drama out in space. The

rope John is tethered to breaks and he starts to float away. Maureen quickly slips on her gear and joins him outside the ship to shoot him a line. It misses. *I'll keep my mouth shut so I wont be thought of as anything less than a full fledged feminist.* What happens as John floats just a few feet from the Jupiter 2? You'll find out as we move on to an unimaginable spaceship, The Derelict.

"The Derelict"

John is floating in space and a comet is headed our way. **Bill Haley can't be too far behind.** Maureen is successful this time as she tosses him another line. He is saved and goes back to work on the scanner. **This is a husband and wife team at its best.** But still, the comet is getting closer, and the heat has enlarged the hull of the ship. The air-lock door won't open, and John and Maureen can't get back inside. Don tries to open the door, but he can't. Young Will comes to the rescue and uses a fire extinguisher to get the door open. *Why didn't I think of that? Shown up by an eleven year old and in front of his pretty sister! I feel embarrassed and don't want to look in her direction. What can I do to save face? I know. I'll pull them into safety and then Pilot the Jupiter 2 away from the comet.*

As Don pulls the ship away, a weird sound is picked up from an approaching spaceship. It is huge. Utterly enormous! **Its size is beyond words but not beyond the Major's words. His line in the script was,** *"It's like nothing I've ever seen before, but it's twice as big."* **Really, if you have never seen it before, how do you know it is twice as big? Can we lose that line? Thanks.** *It's opening up! This ugly looking spaceship is sucking us in! Where the hell is reverse on this stinking spaceship? I can't believe Alpha Control didn't put a reverse in this spacecraft! I'll close my eyes, push some of those pretty colored buttons and hope for the best. Oh, My God, we're not crashing. I did good! I'm a hero! I'll take a peek. I don't believe it. What the hell is happening? We're being swallowed whole, that's what's happening, and are now safely inside this mother of all spaceships.* John and Don decide to find out what this giant spaceship is all about, taking Smith with them. Meanwhile, Will tricks the robot by imitating Dr. Smith's voice and is able to escape the Jupiter 2 to follow the others. Inside the mother spaceship, Will is followed by a huge, bald centipede-like creature and tries to talk to it. **Isn't that what any ten year old boy would do?** Smith comes and shoots at it. **How come he's not still with John and Don and who gave him** a laser? That's a well kept secret! And of course, it attacks back. Will screams and John and Don hurry towards where he and Smith are located. They all race back to the ship. Don prepares for lift off and activates the force field to keep the big creature at bay while John blasts a hole at the entrance of the mother ship. They lift off. **Luck...eee.**

And they got real lucky with that comet, didn't they? The comet got close enough to heat the hull of the ship. But, could a comet do that? Don tells Judy that even if it misses the Jupiter 2 by 5,000 miles, its heat could shrivel them in nothing flat. Now, Don West graduated with the highest honors in science from a distinguished university at the age of twenty. Wouldn't he know that comets are balls of frozen ice? He must have been partying the night before that class about comets. John Robinson, obviously, never missed class and did his homework because his sharp mind sought out the location of an earth-like planet. It is there that they plan to land to make some necessary repairs on the Jupiter 2, and we get to visit an island in the sky.

"Island in the Sky"

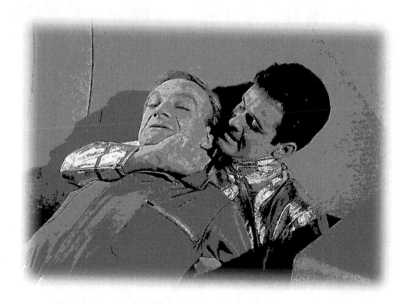

I'll bet John wishes that this adventure was "A pie in the sky." As they approach the planet, John wants to send the robot down to investigate. Smith, however, tampers with the robot so that John is faced to go himself. He never makes it as planned, though, because Smith also tampered with John's parajet thrusters, draining them of fuel in an evil plot to lighten the ship of John's weight in order to get back to earth. John falls helplessly to the planet below as his family and Don watch helplessly from the Jupiter 2. Maureen refuses to believe he is dead. *"Maureen, he fell about 10,000 feet, for God' sake, but I'll take the ship down and try to land as close as possible to where John might be. As*

Don starts the maneuver to land, the Jupiter 2 starts fluctuating wildly due to Smith's earlier interference with the control panel. Shortly after Don stabilizes the ship with Maureen's help, Penny tells them she saw Dr. Smith by the parajet thrusters. When Don finally realizes what happened, he grabs Smith in a neck hold. *"Smith,....I outta...***I can't make this too tight or Jonathan will have a fit. I'll keep my arm under his chin and away from his throat while he makes a face like he can't breath or scream. I sure don't want to hear him scream. I'll make that clenched teeth face that says, look out world, Don West is here.** *"Alright, Smith, I've had it with your crap. I'm gonna wring your neck so tight your eyes will bulge so you'll look like Zar Zar Binks! Besides that, I'm going to put you in a freezing tube with nothing but a popsicle to suck on until we find John in good shape."* With Smith in a freezing tube, Don pilots the ship toward the planet. **You guessed it.** The ship's thrusters don't fire because of Smith's continued tampering, and the Jupiter 2 crash lands. *"I'm sorry, Maureen, something happened to the thrusters. It wasn't a pilot error, I promise."* Oh, well, now she'll never let me take Judy out for a joy ride in the Jupiter!

Now, all of sudden, there is a stored vehicle available enabling us to look for John. Where it came from on the ship or how we assembled it so quickly is beyond me. But, not beyond Don West!

"Okay, everyone, line up and listen. Shoulders back, Will. Chest out, Judy. Good...Okay, now, we have to work fast and as a team if we are to locate John before Christmas.

We have the parts to a glass enclosed tank below deck. I'm calling it a Chariot in honor of Ben Hur, one of my favorite heroes, second only to Curly of the Three Stooges. We will build it in stages. From the bottom up. Got that? Will, go below deck and you will find metal tractor threads that weigh about four tons. Bring them up. And Penny, stop bopping to the Beatles and help him. Maureen, you'll see some round orange colored pipe-like pieces that are more square than round, and they are more reddish orange than orange, I think. There are about sixty pieces in different sizes so could you please sort them out and bring them up from storage. Judy, you bring out the scientific glass blower, and start blowing the windows for the frame. Where is it? You can't miss it. It's about the size of a Volvo. Let's get to work. We've got about twenty minutes to get this done!

Don and the family use the Chariot to search for John. After hearing a blip on the scanner, they enter a small jungle-like area. Don leaves the Chariot and among the foliage he discovers a small creature. *Whoa, what is this? Looks like a chimp with ears like a donkey. I think I'll take it back to the Chariot. I'll look for John later. I can't wait to see the look on Penny's face when she sees this unique specimen of whatever. She loves animals. It makes me wonder why she loves The Beatles more than The Monkees. I'd better hurry, it's getting dark.* Don takes the chimp-like creature back to the Chariot, and it won't leave. Penny keeps it and names it Debbie. **Why the name Debbie? I guess because Penny's full name is Penelope, and maybe she had a favorite aunt named Debelope. Go figure!**

Back in the Chariot, Don uses the scanner and finds that John is trapped in a pit. He hauls John out and they head back to the Jupiter.

Meanwhile, Smith has made another plan to hijack the Jupiter after he reprograms the robot to get rid of the family and Major West by electrical discharge. They'll be killed one at a time, and it will look like an accident. However, when Smith realizes the robot can't fly the spaceship, he decides to keep his nemesis, Major West alive. **Good thinking, Smith, but what makes you think the Red Baron can get you back to Earth without crashing into The Grand Canyon? Snoopy would be a better choice, but he's not part of the group. And, how is the robot going to get them, one by one, alone to kill them? Wait outside the bathroom? I don't think that would work.**

The Chariot is heading back to the spaceship when a huge plant-like-thing rolls by. **Irwin must have a hell of a garden at his house.** It sucks the power from the Chariot and the crew has to walk back to the Jupiter. They confront Smith because of all his tampering. As usual, the devious Smith manages to cover his tracks and elude any consequences. **Come on guys, can you be that stupid?** After supper, Will goes out to try to fix the Chariot... Alone! **I guess John and Don didn't notice because they were too busy sipping their after dinner cordials and enjoying their Cuban cigars or they are that stupid.** The robot follows. **There is tension in the air just before they discover there were giants in the earth.**

"There Were Giants in the Earth"

Will is alone and the robot tries to kill him, because of the evil plan Dr. Smith devised to get rid of the Robinson family. It was all in vain, though, as Will is too smart and imitates Smith's voice to foil the deadly plot. Luckily, John and Don arrive and make Smith deactivate the robot. Unbelievably, Smith only gets a "slap on the wrist" warning because John isn't sure the problem was deliberate. *Deliberate? This man is evil, and we better do something about him before we all*

end up in no man's land. Oh, that's where we are now. Well, it could get worse. Don't ask me why I feel this way, but I sense that no good is coming down the pike. Or, the Milky Way for that matter.

The next day the Robinsons set up camp. Judy and Penny start planting seeds. **Good girl work!** John and Don set up the the force field generator. **Good man work!** Will repairs the radio telescope. **Good boy work.** Maureen prepares a hearty, healthy meal for all the workers. **Good woman work.** Smith doesn't do anything. **Good laggard work!** But, eventually, he agrees to plant some seeds that turn into monsters the next day. **What would you expect coming from the consummate bad seed?**The monsters have tentacles and attack, but Will uses his laser to stop them. **"Never fear, Will is near" is much more appropriate than "Never fear, Smith is here!"** John and Don examine what's left of the monsters and discover strange alien micro-organisms. *That was more interesting than cutting up frogs in my tenth grade biology class which I nearly failed when I snuck two legs home to saute' with garlic and lemon juice and enjoy with a bottle of Moxie.*

Later that day, Will secretly reprograms the robot while John and Don repair the Chariot. **Anything that distracts the adults is fine as long as Will can do his thing without being noticed. This time, though doing his thing didn't turn out so hot.** Because of Will's tinkering, the robot's wires got messed up. So, now, the robot doesn't respond too well to orders, and that night it hears a noise and turns off the force field in order to investigate. **Why the heck did we set the force field up?** He returns muttering some nonsense about twenty foot humanoids. John assumes the robot is just overworked. *"Come on, John. It hasn't done diddle dee. Look at its claws. Do you see any callouses? And if you mean its circuits are overloaded, how can that be? It wasn't sent to us by Sears and Roebuck. Or maybe it was. It seems a little clumsy and overweight for Alpha Control to have developed."*

Overweight is something Alpha Control would have been very strict about. By all accounts, Smith's added weight on the Jupiter 2 was enough to throw us off course in the first place. It was calibrated so that we could lift off with just the right amount of weight on board. I never bought this and think the weight factor was a scapegoat for Alpha Control in case the ship did a belly flop into the Atlantic Ocean. Otherwise, we could have spared 175 pounds considering all the junk we brought along.

The next day, John and Don head out to the weather station and discover a severe cold spell is headed their way. The temperature is about to drop to 150 degrees below zero. **That, my friend, is climate change!** John says they have to get out of there and head south as soon as possible. *Sounds great to me! I'll get to show off my new speedo bathing suit to Judy.* **Not so fast, speedo Don-galas.**

Don spots a giant footprint. *"Can you believe the size of that footprint, John? It's like nothing I've ever seen before, but twice as big!"* **For Pete's sake, Don, that line doesn't**

make sense, remember? All of a sudden, a giant cyclops emerges and traps them in a cave. Will, seeing the trouble they're in on the Jupiter's radio telescope, takes a laser pistol and runs to the mountainous area. His aim is perfect, and he stuns the one-eyed monster with his laser gun.

When they return, the family quickly begins to load up the Chariot to head south because of the dropping temperatures when they notice Penny is suddenly missing. John dons **(or is it Don John's?)** the jet pack to locate her. She decided to take her oversized turtle for a ride. John was able to catch up with her, and Penny gets a faster ride home by piggybacking with her dad on the para jet. They leave for their picnic area in space without Smith and the robot who will ride the cold weather out in the Jupiter.

On their way, they encounter another Cyclops **Or maybe its his twin sister.** *"Let me get it, John."* *Try to kill me with a stinking tree, will ya? I'll show you who's boss now, you hairy, one eyed bully. Damn, how do ya' open up this bubble gun hatch thing? Oh,oh. He's got another boulder over his head. I've only got a few seconds to aim my laser rifle. But where?* *"Judy, help me open this hatch, will ya'? Never mind, I've got it."* *Go for the eye. That looks like a bullseye target. One for the money, two for the show, three to get ready and four to go! Aim... and fire. Missed. But I hit her somewhere...she's falling...toward us! Whoa, she missed hitting us. That was a real bad landing. I wonder if her name is Mae Cyclops West?* **Don only wanted to blind the little lady, but in good old Don West fashion, he**

missed the target. They drive by the monster with morbid curiosity. *Wherever I got her, it worked. How come no one is congratulating me? They're all looking at this ugly cyclops monster with sympathy. I don't get it. Where's the sympathy for me when I'm the victim, which is usually the situation.*

That night, they camp out, and Don is able to be alone with Judy for awhile. He's working under the Chariot, while she seductively sits near him. *I've never been in such an unusual romantic situation before. I'm flat on my back with little room to move and grease all over me. What'll I say? I could start by asking her to hand me the solar wrench, and when she does I can grab her hand and kiss it. No, the solar wrench might get in the way and I could break a tooth. I could ask her to join me. But for what reason? To look at the underbelly of the Chariot? That's stupid. Be smart for once in your life. Make meaningful eye contact. First, get her attention. Clear your throat. No response, huh. Do it, again. Nothing. Judy, look under here... stop gazing at Will and his guitar. Good. She's adjusting to get more comfortable. She's putting her hand on the ground within my reach. This is the moment! I'll gently take her hand, raise it slightly off the ground and kiss it. Yes! Nice move. That was easy. Oh, oh, Penny saw the kiss and is going over to Maureen. I can see that this is going to be a kiss free adventure in space.*

The next day a violent electrical storm strikes. **Looks like that kiss set off sparks all over this planet.** Everyone leaves the Chariot with their flashlights and seek shelter in a nearby cave. **Good thinking, gang,**

caves are usually pretty dark. Don takes Debbie and
they enter the cob-webbed cave. **The reason Don is in
charge of the Bloop (the alternate name for Debbie)
is because she bit Penny's finger earlier. I guess she
was angry, because Penny was dressing her in awful
girlie outfits. With all the things we brought from
earth for our journey, you'd think Alpha Control
would have let Penny take her Barbie doll with her
fancy wardrobe.**

Debbie wanders off. **Don did a lousy job of
baby-sitting Debbie!** Will and Penny follow
Debbie and discover a secret passageway. **A secret
passageway always spells trouble.** They get trapped
in a mummified room. Then Don and Judy, looking
for them, also get trapped there when the secret
passageway stone door shuts behind them. *"Don't
anyone panic! Your parents aren't trapped in here yet, so
don't panic. I know it's dark Penny, but our flashlights are
equipped with Eveready batteries that are guaranteed to last
5,000 hours, so just stay calm. No, Penny, we won't be in
here that long! We didn't take our solar walkie talkies Will,
so we will have to communicate the old fashioned way. We'll
yell. We'll take turns so as not to confuse your dad and
mom. I'll go first. John!! Maureen !! It's me, Don! I have
the kids, and we are behind an unmarked stone doorway.
When you find it, if you find it, laser blast our way out of
here. Good Luck, and this is an actual vocal so there'll be
no '"over and out." What's happening now? Feels like an
earthquake or maybe one of those giant cyclops is doing a
Fred Astaire tap dancing routine.*

Okay, an earthquake. That means everyone has to fall to the left and then to the right as Irwin hits the tin film holder with his drum stick and tells the actors to make it look real. Being a method actor, I'll do a sense memory to make it look real. I'll work on the last time I had too much to drink and couldn't stand up. *Wow! This is dangerous stuff. Pillars are falling down, the earth is moving and cracking beneath my feet, and dirt and cobwebs are getting in my hair which is really pissing me off. I hear John. "Hallelujah! We're saved!! Blast away, John! Go for it...Get us out...Rocks are falling down all around us. Do your thing! Take aim and shoot the freakin' laser!! You're the man! Just do it!! What's taking you so long?"* Outside the room where Don, Judy, Will and Penny are trapped, John tries to burn through the blocks with his laser. Can he do it in time? *"Yes! He's doing it!"* John finally cuts through the blocks and the family is reunited. **How about that!** *How about this? Hugs and kisses for everybody except the Major. I am feeling distanced from this warm, loving family. Debbie, the Bloop, I think is feeling my pain, too. She purses her big lips when I'm holding her. But no, I can't take advantage of her compassionate proposal, no matter how isolated I might feel. Things are bound to get better although Debbie is getting to look awfully cute to me as time passes. I just have to keep telling myself that I'll get over this obsessive loneliness.* **Don't worry, Don, you won't feel lonely once you reach the hungry sea.**

"The Hungry Sea"

The family makes it back to the Chariot. Back at the Jupiter, the robot comes up with some weird calculations about the peculiar orbit of this new planet. The temperature has dropped to 125 below zero. *That's cold, man. That's colder than a witch's you know what. And if you don't know what, forget I had the thought.* The Chariot reaches the sea which is completely iced over. *This is cool. Break out the ice skates!* They cross to land.

Meanwhile, Dr. Smith is suddenly worried about the space family because if they perish he would be left all alone. **What a change in attitude! First, he wants to kill them all, and now he wants to save them. Well, the show must go on.** He sends the robot after the Robinsons with a message of impending doom. Don thinks it's a trick and shoots the robot. **A little impulsive? Maybe, but Don has a cowboy mentality and he believes in shooting first and asking questions later.** Will pleads with his dad to let him restore the Robot. *I wish that kid, once in awhile, would mind his own business.* John relents and lets Will fix the nefarious ninny. He also finds the message, and Don is pretty embarrassed. The message says they are about to be hit with a heat wave, and although Don thinks it is a mistake, he helps the clan get ready for it. Don was wrong. It gets hellishly hot. They cover themselves with protective sheets, but they're of little help so they sweat it out before preparing to back to the Jupiter on the same boat that got them here. **Boat? The Chariot becomes a boat because the ice melted, and now the family has to travel across water.** *Thank God I made the Chariot amphibious when we assembled it! My idea of putting all the stored recreational winter and summer floating tubes under the belly of the Chariot turned out to be pretty prophetic, after all.*

Everything went well until they came upon a whirlpool. At that point, Judy implored John to cut to the left. It didn't help. If she had told him to cut to the right, we might have been saved, but it was

a poor judgement call. They were stuck without power in the middle of a whirlpool. *"John, it must be a solar battery. I'll go topside and fix it." I've got to get this right because Judy will be watching my every move. Wow, it's windy and moist up here. In fact, the waves are crashing over the Chariot. I'll crawl to the scanner and hold onto it so I won't be washed over. Let's see now, this must be the scanner. It's the only thing up here. There are a lot of bolts attached. I'd better get my solar wrench. I'll call to Judy to hand it to me through the hatch. "Judy, hand me the solar wrench...No. Those are the solar pliers! Wrench!! Wrench!!! NO. I'm not calling you a wench, for goodness sake... Thanks! "I'm getting soaked up here! Stay cool ole buddy, remember, Judy's watching. Boy, there are a lot of screws on this scanner. Damn, it is the solar pliers I need, after all, not the solar wrench. Heck, I'll just use the solar wrench and bang the hell out of the scanner. Whoa, another wave almost knocked me over. I better get back inside. "I got it fixed! I'm coming back, open the hatch!!" Eeeeeeeee...I'm not coming back. I'm going overrrrrrrr. That wave got me real good. Thank God I grabbed the ladder and held on for dear life. And thank the Lord that He gave me the reflexes of Quasimodo. I can hear Judy calling my name. She cares! She really cares!! That's all the motivation I need to get back up the ladder and to the hatch. What? They closed the stupid hatch because of a little water? I'll pound on it. I'm sorry that you guys have to get all wet, but I need to get in!!* **Judy pulls him, head first, into the Chariot, with tons of water following him. It was like Neptune's daughter's water broke and out came**

Don West. Looking like a soaked bunny rabbit, Don still managed a grin. The Chariot is powered again. *What the hell did I do to make this crate run again? And, with only my solar wrench, it really was a miracle!* They all make it to the Jupiter 2. Things are finally getting back to normal when Smith sees something on the radar. Well, things have to move on even if we're not ready to greet someone with a "Welcome, stranger."

"Welcome Stranger"

A spaceship named "Travelin' Man" lands not too far from the Jupiter 2, and a cowboy spaceman dismounts. His name is Jimmy Hapgood and it looks like he traded his horse in for a space craft.

When I read the script "Welcome Stranger," I liked it. When I heard that Warren Oates was to play the part of Hapgood, I was excited to have *the* opportunity to work with such an accomplished actor. He was outstanding in The Wild Bunch back in 1960, and he appeared with me in an episode of Johnny Ringo. So, like myself, he had the spirit of the old West in his blood.

Will, acting like a space diplomat, befriends the grungy looking cowboy and helps him decontaminate his one man vehicle. But, they missed some spots, and some microorganisms start to grow. **Will, of course, brings the buckaroo back to the spaceship to meet the family and treat him to a home cooked meal. Everyone is hospitable to him except Don who gives him the once over, twice.** *I don't know about this. Judy might be attracted to this rascally looking fellow. He's single, independent minded and speaks with a western twang. Women like accents whether it's British, Cockney or Southern. Just as long as it's not a Boston accent. I had better keep my eye on him to make sure I'm not his "hound dog."*

According to Hapgood, he left Earth in 1982 to make a landing on Saturn, but he missed it. *Okay, cowboy, you missed Saturn? Maybe you should have headed in the other direction and aimed for the planet Jupiter. How could you miss that? I wouldn't miss it. I might crash on it, but I sure as hell wouldn't have missed it.*

The script gets a little complicated when John thinks we can help Hapgood return to Earth. John and Maureen want him to take Will and Penny back with him. Naturally, Smith wants to use Hapgood's ship if the journey is at all possible. The cowboy nixes taking the kids and scolds John for even thinking of such a proposition. This leads to fisticuffs between Don and Hapgood. *I can take this puny looking John Wayne wannabe. Jab, jab...dance around a little...jab, jab.. oops, I almost fell down. He's pretty quick in those cowboy boots, but I can still take him. Judy's watching so I've got to look good! Jab, jab...shuffle a little. Ooh, he got me in the ribs. That hurt, and I'm getting tired. I'll grab him and hold* *on. Yeah, the rope-a- dope, like how Muhammad Ali use to box.* John breaks up the fight and nothing is resolved. **Why is Don always getting himself into jams he can't get out of or into fights he can't win? I guess he better stick with the cowardly Smith and be glad they changed Jonathan's character from a military saboteur to an obnoxious wimp.**

After Hapgood refuses Jonathan's offer of disassembled robot parts to help him return to Earth, he takes Will and Penny out to his ship. It is now covered by plants evolved from the microorganisms they missed killing. Penny is grabbed by a plant, but she is pulled free by Hapgood. Will again saves the day with his decontaminating spray gun. The cowboy now likes the kids and agrees to take them with him. But Smith, the troublemaker, works to thwart the plan because he wants to be the passenger on the "Travelin' Man." He talks Will and Penny into running away, and they hide. Hapgood then changes his mind about going back to Earth and decides to roam where the buffalo don't for the rest of his natural life. **Good luck, cowboy, and maybe you'll get to meet my friend, Mr. Nobody.**

"My Friend Mr. Nobody"

I love being on the set as this show progresses. How great it is to see Angela have the chance to demonstrate her acting ability. Believe me, she is talented and is excellent in one of the better episodes of *Lost in Space*. The script is imaginative as written by Jackson Gillis and very well directed by Paul Stanley. John Williams, who composed theme music for our series, also contributed incidental music for this particular episode.

John and Don are drilling (**what else**) for material to be used as fuel. They are about to set off an explosion just as Penny wanders into the area. **It looks like Penny likes to wander, whether with or without a turtle to carry her. For a young lass, she is really independent and gets around.** Boom! The explosive goes off, and John saves her life. *Good job, John. If she were my daughter, I would have done the same. Well, she's not my daughter. If she were, she would be listening to tapes made by "The Who" instead of "The Beatles" and wouldn't be wandering around because she got so bored with the banal shouts of "Yeah, Yeah, Yeah." But let that go. Thank God she is safe. I like her an awful lot, and her attitude during this tumultuous flight has a calming effect on me when I get riled up because of Smith. Plus, she is very pretty, and as far as I'm concerned if she were ten years older she'd give Judy a run for her money.*

After this incident, Penny returns to the spaceship. Feeling ignored, she wanders off again. She casually discovers a pool of water, and being thirsty, she kneels to take a sip only to be shocked as the water magically rises to her lips. At the same time, a voice rings out from a nearby cave. Penny enters it.

Now, you would think that she'd learned a lesson about entering caves after she and Will got trapped in a cave during a previous adventure. Anyway, Penny goes in, and a large rock closes behind her. Better luck this time, though, as she is able to leave.

Back at the campsite, Penny's experience falls on deaf ears. Everyone thinks she is making up a story. This upsets her so much that she returns to the cave the next day. **You have good reason to be upset, Penny. Anyone who doesn't believe that the pool of water you drank from works like a drinking fountain or you made contact with a bodiless voice just doesn't have any common sense. Will proved that when** he said that you were talking to Mr. Nobody. To tell you the truth, I think common sense for all the Robinsons and Don went out the porthole when Dr. Smith and the robot joined us, long before your friend Mr. Nobody showed up.

Back in the cave, Penny is teaching her new friend how to talk. Mr. Nobody, as she now calls him, gives her some gems as a gesture of friendship. **I wish I had friends like that. These little rock-like crystals turn out to be diamonds. I wonder who that will interest?** Once Smith discovers that diamonds can be obtained, he tries to convince Penny to take him to the location, but she refuses his request. So Smith and the robot follow Penny to the cave on her next visit. Unable to enter the cave, as Penny did, Smith listens through a hole to the voice of Mr. Nobody. He tells Penny that he has been around for millions of years and is still learning and growing. **Maybe there is hope for Dr. Smith, after all. But can you imagine putting up with an insufferable person like him for even three years?** Smith wants the diamonds, and he is able to get Don to agree to blast open the cave by lying that there is fuel material there. **Don must have chug-a-lugged an unearthed bottle of whisky left by the cowboy, Hapgood, to go along with Smith's outlandish plea.**

Meanwhile, at the ship, Maureen is telling Penny that she also had a not so real friend when she was little. **Nice try, Maureen, but I don't think Penny is in any frame of mind to hear about Howdy Doody.** Once Will tells her that Smith and Don are out blasting,

Penny puts two and two together, comes up with five, and is off to the races. Once there, she goes to warn her friend but is knocked cold when the explosives go off. **That's two for two in two days (which also comes out to five) for our pretty Miss Penny Robinson.** Mr. Nobody thinks she is dead and creates a ball of energy that goes after Don and Smith. *"That was a brilliant idea, Smith." Come on feet, do your thing! "Why did I listen to you?" I'm getting stupider by the minute. "If we get through this, if we ever do, I'm going to send you to the moon just the way Ralph Kramden always threatened to do to Alice."*

Don and Smith make it back to the spaceship. The robot tries to halt the angry energized force but is ripped apart by it. Then Penny shows up after suffering a slight concussion. She calms Mr. Nobody, and is very sad when her friend leaves for outer space to join other forces that make up all the galaxies. Smith finishes fixing the robot, but he is totally unaware that he is being watched by invaders from the fifth dimension.

"Invaders From The Fifth Dimension"

The title of this episode really grabbed me. Why fifth dimension? Were these invaders about to sing "The Age of Aquarius?" My research tells me that the fifth dimension is three spacial dimensions and used to explain the location of supernatural phenomena, events etc. They should have just called the episode, "Weirdos from another Dimension."

There's a blip on the radar screen, seen by the ever vigilant Judy. *"It's probably nothing, Judy. We get blips all the time. I'll bet Penny is playing "The Beatles" on her tape machine, and they hit another sour note."* **Not this time, Major West. This is for real or surreal as it turns out to be.** An alien spacecraft that looks like a giant eyeball on legs lands not too far from the Jupiter 2. The inhabitants of the spaceship spot Smith, who is outside loafing. When the dawdling doctor spots them, he runs as fast as he can to get away from the aliens. **His "fast" is like watching a Sumo Wrestler doing the backstroke in an empty pool.** They are able to freeze him. It seems that they need to replace a bad computer **(I guess Radio Shack hasn't opened yet)**, and a human brain will do as a replacement. But, Smith's brain is too big, so he volunteers Will's smaller brain as a substitute. They agree and put a collar on Smith that will strangle him if he double-crosses them. **Before "think" became "thunk", why didn't Don think of that?**

Smith, who is under the watchful eyes of the aliens, finds Will, who is out rock hunting. **Good hobby for a kid who lives on a desert.** The deceitful doctor manufactures yet another lie, and Will goes off with him to the alien ship. John and Maureen take the chariot to look for Will after they think that Smith has been acting strangely. **But, doesn't he always?** Don gets to put on the Jet Pack, and goes for a ride so he can look for Will. *What a view! This is a lot of fun, but how the heck do you land safely in one of these? I'd better find a soft tree somewhere.*

While they are looking, the aliens take Will and free Smith. John, Maureen, and the robot, come across Smith. Don joins them. **I guess they were able to get Don untangled and down from a look-a-like coconut tree!** They head for the alien spaceship. The aliens fire at the robot, damaging it and open fire on the family. *Not again? What good is this round, metallic, rubberized thing? Whenever we need him, he falls apart like an overcooked duck.* The four would be rescuers are immobilized. Will says he will run the alien's computer if they let his family go. During the process, he sees his mother on the screen, and his emotions overwhelm him. This causes the computer power to overload, demolishing the alien spacecraft. The family escapes and is saved. *I could swear, though, that I could hear the aliens from the fifth dimension singing their hit song of 1967, "Up, up and away," as they left the planet.* **They're lucky they left, because it is getting too damn hot and soon we'll be looking for the oasis.**

"The Oasis"

Water is very scarce. The members of the Jupiter 2 are down to a pint a day. **If it were whisky, Don probably wouldn't have cared about what Dr. Smith ended up doing.** He took a shower, with the help of the robot, and just about emptied the reserve tank. *"I don't believe it, John! Why I outta...You mean Smith really used the last of our water supply to wash his ugly body? We have to waterboard him, John. That's what we gotta do! He wants water? Let's give him water! Oh, yeah, we don't have any. Then let's waterboard him with sand. God knows, we have plenty of that!"*

The family search an old dried up river bed for any signs of water when they come across a stagnant pool. It has foliage with a fruit-looking growth connected to it which they take back to analyze. John thinks the fruit might help their thirst because of the moisture it contains. **Bad move, John. If the fruit is poisonous, it could prove very dangerous if the kids are tempted.** *Good move, John. If the fruit is poisonous, we know who would be the first to disobey instructions not to eat it.* But, Debbie, the monkey, is the first to eat one. Then of course, Smith, the glutton, eats a couple. He thinks John and Don have poisoned him out of revenge for wasting our water supply. He leaves the ship, playing the victim. Will cries and everyone is saddened except for John and Don. *"Yeah! Get lost!! Get lost in the desert. Saves me a lot of trouble thinking of ways to get rid of you."* Smith leaves taking the final fuel cell with him. *So cry me a river, Will.*

The next morning, father and son, along with a cynical Don, go looking for Smith. *I don't believe we are doing this unless we want to hunt him down and kill him.* Back at the ship, Debbie has grown to man-size. If Debbie, then guess who? Bingo! When they find Smith, he is about thirty feet tall. *This is scary! Wow! And he is pissed off! He's ripping a tree up by its roots. Its Cyclops all over again, but we don't have a cave to hide in! Will, for crying out loud, do something. He's your buddy, so say something before we all end up like baseballs being batted by the trunk of that tree!* Smith throws the tree at them. Will tries to calm him down but to no avail. Finally, Maureen shows up and makes him feel like a hero by having him think he only tried the fruit to make sure it was safe for the rest of us.

That night the sky is falling with rain, and Debbie and Smith shrink back to normal size.

"The Sky is Falling"

Smith, back to his old self, is sleeping on the desert sand when a strange looking mechanical thing wakes him up. He panics and runs back to the spaceship. **He always runs when panicked if he doesn't have Will to hide behind.** This thing, with a big claw, somehow transfers itself inside the ship. After an investigation, it's thought to be some kind of mobile computer that is testing the environment. *It looks more like a mutated, futuristic lobster to me.* Will, through his radio telescope, sees a beam of light and in it is a small saucer-shaped machine which is a matter-transfer contraption. A man, a woman and a boy appear beside it. The Curious and devious Dr. Smith sets the lobster free and follows it back to the alien camp. He wants, of course to make a deal with the father of the family, who cannot speak a language. This frightens Smith, and he pulls his laser on them. **How the hell did Smith ever get his hands on a laser?** But the man gets his own gun, and Smith backs down. **I don't think Smith would ever show up at *High Noon*.** Back at the Jupiter, Smith warns the family that these are only the first arrivals, and soon aliens will be everywhere. **What is he afraid of? Someone taking his job at the hydroponic garden? Or taking his room on the Jupiter 2?** Nobody is impressed with his concerns and ignore him.

Will goes out to the alien camp and makes friends with the young son. The boy unexpectedly collapses, and Will takes him to a nearby cave. **We sure have a lot of caves on this desert we call home.** The mothers are worried about their sons and have everyone looking for them. This is another chance for Smith to cause trouble, so he lies about the aliens taking Will. As the boys aren't found, the next morning John, Don and Smith arrive at the alien camp with their lasers. *I've got my trusty laser pistol on my right hip and I'm ready to go if trouble occurs.* John tries to talk to the mute father without any luck. Smith fires at the mother when he sees her with a gun. *Nice going, Dum-Dum. Why you still have a gun is beyond me, but you do and I'm glad you're as bad a shot as I am.* John, Don, and Smith take cover but shots aren't fired because Will, shows up and demonstrates his friendship with the ailing alien.

The alien boy contracted germs from Will, and that was the reason he got sick. The aliens communicate, finally, by radio waves and leave, realizing they can't co-exist because of cross infecting each other, on a planet with the Robinsons. **If, in their travels they pick up some nasty germs, they can always wish upon a star for better health.**

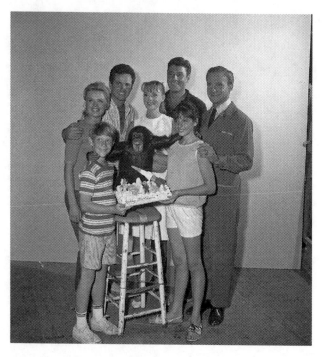

A birthday celebration early on in the first season

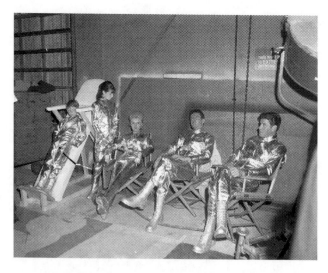

Relaxing between takes

Getting ready to tour Beverly Hills in my fiat

Taken just before the cop stopped me on
Coldwater Canyon in Beverly Hills

Who has the biggest smile?

Trying to control the ship right after I was thawed out

A rare shot with the viewport glass removed

An on-screen romance that never got to blossom

Christmas party on set with
Director Sobey Martin
We were filming the
Keeper at this time.

My daughter Melissa and I
visiting with Adam West at
20th Century Fox Studios

Enjoying some champagne
with Ryan O'Neal and
Susan Oliver at a 20th
Century Fox event

Guy and I share a laugh on the set

Here's Guy and I after being interviewed
for a magazine article

Hands on hip – no belt

This was taken so 20th could make cut-
outs of all of us for the studio tours

Marta and I posing for third season publicity shots

Marta and I relaxing between takes during the
filming of the episode "A Visit to a Hostile Planet"

This is when the Allman
Brothers were invited
to the set by June. They
were known as the Hour
Glass at this time

Jonathan and I mugging
between takes during
the filming of
"Princess of Space"

That's the talented Michael
Conrad during the filming
of "Fugitives in Space"

Billy and I during the filming of "The Flaming Planet."
Feeling like a cowboy with that gun belt.

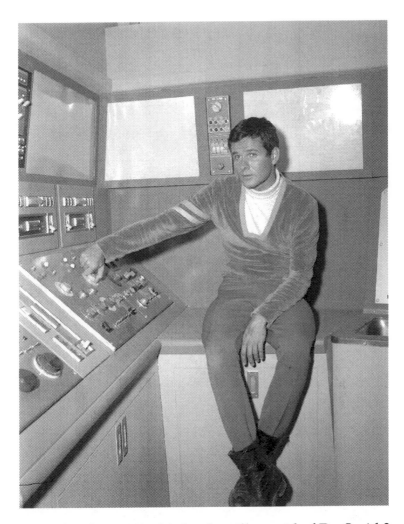

I wonder if turning this knob will get rid of Dr. Smith?

A typical CBS promo slide where they
always seemed to reverse the image

"Wish Upon a Star"

Some time later, Don and Will are working on the Chariot while Smith looks on. *I like it this way. I can keep an eye on him, and as long as he watches and doesn't touch anything we should be okay.* "That's a fuel tank, Smith, so don't try to pick it up. Don't pick it up! Smith drops the fuel tank and it explodes. *"Why I outta...You stupid, clumsy jerk! What's the matter with you? First, you destroy the hydroponic garden and now, our fuel tank! You're out of here. Smith, I don't care where the hell you go, just get out of my sight! I'll explain to John and he'll agree that you are too much of a liability to be just hanging around, which is all you do when not causing trouble. Oh, so now you want to leave? Good! And good riddance!!"*

Smith camps out in the desert and is spooked by his own imagination of nighttime ghouls. In the morning, Will finds him, and they look for a place for him to stay. **Why is it that Will is always looking out for Smith? What mysterious influence and control does this incompetent, evil man have over this bright, fine, young boy?** They discover an old spaceship and clean it out. While doing this, Will finds a strange looking metal cap. Thinking how hungry he is, some food appears. He thinks about what he would love to have as a food item, and apples fall from above. **I wonder if Sir Isaac Newton was wearing a metal wish cap when an apple fell from a tree, hit him on the head while he was sleeping, and led to his theory of gravity?**

The cap makes wishes come true. Smith, of course, dominates the use of the cap and turns the old space ship into a comfortable home for himself. Delicacies, fine wines and a soft comfortable bed are among the things he materializes because of the wish cap. Will is disappointed in Smith's selfishness **(Where have you been all year, Will?)** and rats him out to his dad. Smith gives in to his young friend and his father and returns to the Jupiter 2 with the magical wish cap. Smith tries to wish for a second space ship to get him back to Earth, but it only produces a miniature model. **I'll bet that miniature model will make a great collectible some day.** Also, Smith discovered that the cap will only work twice a day. Now, greed raises its ugly head and causes conflict among the youngsters . Will and

Penny argue over turns. Penny cheats to get more *Beatles* music tapes, and Judy wishes for a new dress and takes Don Juan off for a walk. **You can guess what Don wished for.** John is fed up with the laziness and selfishness being displayed by his family and orders Smith to get rid of the machine.

Smith returns to the "wish" ship to live like a king. He tries to create a servant but wakes the captain of the ship who wants his machine back. Smith, frightened as usual, runs back to the Jupiter 2. When he arrives, he discovers that the machine has a time limit. Judy's dress is in ruins, and all the food is rotting. Smith sets up a force field to keep the alien space crewman at bay, but John commands him to give up the wish cap. Smith does so, reluctantly. The alien then retrieves his machine and goes back home but not before leaving Will Robinson an apple. **Remember Will, an apple a day keeps the doctor away. Don might say to that, *"Don't I WISH!"* And when Will was experimenting with rockets to send rescue messages into space, maybe he should have wished for something to get us off this planet like the raft.**

"The Raft"

Will's messenger rocket explodes dangerously near the Jupiter 2 campsite. No more rockets, says dad even though little is said about the use of the last of our fuel supply. But who needs fuel when John and Don have been toying with the idea of plasma motors. They experiment with the idea, and it apparently works. The family and Smith are excited and all fingers are crossed when they hook it into the ship's system to give it a try. *"Okay, guys, this may be the moment. We*

might finally get this old crate off the ground and into the *wild blue yonder."* Just push the right buttons, and off we'll go! Keep pushing, baby. Keep pushing! Okay, let's try some other buttons. Come on! I can hear a little whirring. How about a little more juice? Push the buttons harder! Let's go!!! Sounds like a pregnant cow in breech mode. This isn't going to work. "You can uncross your fingers. This is a no go. We're not getting enough power to launch a lawnmower. Back to the drawing board. What's that Will? Maybe we can try a smaller craft, like a raft? Sounds daffy but let's give it a try."

This turns out to be a brilliant idea. Think of it for a minute. The raft will be lifted by a balloon, and when it is way up in the air, you'll start the motors. *You will? You mean... I will. "I don't remember volunteering for this mission." Don't look at me like that, Judy. I'd like to enjoy another birthday, maybe have kids and maybe kiss a girl again. Don't purse your lovely lips like that. "Okay, I'll do it." After all, I like to think of myself as fearless Don West, and the only thing I have to fear is death.*

John has programmed the raft to navigate itself back to Earth. Judy comes by Don's room to wish him good luck. *God, she's pretty. I'm pretty too. Pretty scared about this whole whacky idea of a balloon raft in space.* **Don should realize that the trip will never take place. Not with Smith around to mess it up.** That night, Smith and the robot are in the raft when Will enters it to talk to Dr. Smith. The robot, on a signal from the agitator Smith, releases the balloon. They land in the desert on the same planet they left from. To make life more interesting, some plants chase them around and after making radio contact, John and Don come to the rescue. They burn down the bush-like creature that has been threatening Will and Smith. **How else to destroy a bush-like creature? Just another sunny day in space but not a sunny day for the ladies when they discover one of our dogs is missing.**

"One of Our Dogs is Missing"

On that sunny day, John, Don, Will and the robot take the Chariot to set up an antenna. **It's always good to have a foursome in case you pass a golf course on the way.** The Chariot is hit by a meteor storm. **That kills golf for the day.**

The storm knocks out the Chariot's communication. Maureen is worried so she and the girls, along with Smith, head out to look for the Chariot. **Make sense? Not really, but it gets them out of the house.** They somehow contact John and find out that the foursome's mission is back on track.

That night, the ladies **(that includes Smith)** hear ghastly howling around the ship. The next morning, the bravest of the brave go out to investigate the source of the howling. **Smith didn't quite make the squad.** They find a very small dog which Penny adopts. Unbeknownst to them, about the same time, a monster with fangs emerges from a bog. Back at the ship, Smith is convinced that the dog is a spy and tries to talk to it. **I'm surprised he didn't try to eat it. It's a good thing he didn't because this is where the fun begins.** Penny is playing with the dog when it grabs a laser and runs off with it. **Maybe he thought it was a fetch toy.** To make the family's lives as impossible as possible, Smith takes all the other guns apart to clean them. **How's that for a "take charge guy"?** But, since he can't put them together, **(No kidding!)** now they have no weapons. Penny searches for the dog, and the fanged monster shows up and follows her. Just in time, the dog arrives and scares off the monster. **Now, either that cute, little dog frightened off that big, scary monster, or the monster sniffed out better prey to follow. I guess the latter.** Judy sets out to look for the dog, and now the monster follows her **(like I said, better prey!).**

John and Don return to the ship. When they learn what happened, John and Don take off to search for Judy. Staying back, Will reassembles the lasers. **(Nothing to it.)** He, Smith and the robot go off in pursuit of the dog who they think is an alien spy in order to kill it. **Are you with me? Getting pretty darn intriguing, don't you think?** In the meantime, the monster chases Judy, and the dog fetches John and Don so they can display their heroics. **Sure they can!**

The monster beats John up. Judy faints. **And Don? I guess he's doing his best Muhammed Ali shuffle imitation.** John comes around and finally shoots the monster. They don't know that he's only stunned, so they go off again looking for the dog who took off during the scuffle. **You'd think the dog was the Holy Grail! Now, comes the showdown.** The monster goes back to the bog. Will has found the dog there, but can't shoot it. **I suppose that he remembers the saying, "Dog is a man's best friend," even if he is an alien spy, as Smith believes.** Everyone is at the bog, and the monster attacks them. *This could have been such a nice night out! But this monster has to ruin everything.* Judy faints again, John is knocked down again, and the dog recovers Will's laser so that Will and John can shoot at the monster and force it back into his bog. **If you're wondering what Don was doing while all this was going on, I don't recall. He certainly was quiet. He might have comforted Judy. He might have tripped over John's body on his way to her. And, he might have been practicing the shuffle before going after the monster. At any rate, They all survived, but can they survive the attack of the monster plants?**

"Attack of the Monster Plants"

After not having a lot to do in the first season, Marta Kristin has the opportunity in the second season "to blossom" (no pun intended) into the wonderful performer we all know her to be. John and Don are snared into a quicksand pit when drilling for fuel. Smith is with them, but he panics and goes to get Will. **Don recalls this experience in the "John and Don show" story.** They are saved by Will and his lasso. Back safely, they kick Smith off the ship for his cowardice. **I don't think the boys care for quicksand.** Before leaving, the ever conniving Smith steals a canister of fuel for bargaining if needed some day. That day comes right away when he discovers a giant cyclamen plant that can produce the illusion of matter outside itself while still being a plant on the inside. Smith tries to switch his canister with one that the plant has materialized. It backfires. The plant loves the fuel and drinks it all. Smith has nothing to bargain with.

That night, Judy is out taking a walk. **Don went to bed early, exhausted, I suppose, from all the running around and fighting he didn't do while looking for that lovable mutt.** She wanders some distance from the campsite when she comes upon one of the cyclamen plants. The plant holds her spellbound, and she crawls inside it to take a quick nap. **Why not?** Smith sees this incident, and his evil mind goes to work. He shows up at the ship the next day and threatens not to tell where Judy is unless he and Don are able to leave and return to Earth. *"Are you kidding me, Smith? If Judy is hurt or disappears, I'll rip out your gizzard and feed it to the robot!!* But violence is prevented when the illusionary plant Judy shows up. She acts a little weird but is apparently all right. She won't eat and won't let Don near her. *"What's going on with you, Judy? I'm not looking for anything from you that I know I can't have, so tell me what's making you behave in this strange way."* Okay, no response. I'll sleep on it and see if she feels better in the morning.

But that morning, the illusionary Judy steals some fuel and feeds it to the plants. Smith gets involved and lies to the illusionary Judy in order to get some of her stolen fuel, but she continues to feed it to the plants. With this fuel source, the plants overrun the ship. John and Don are able to get outside to use the neutron gun in the Chariot to clear the plants away, but the illusionary Judy destroys the gun, revealing that she is the plant creature. *Boy, am I relieved! Can you imagine being lost with a mean-spirited Judy instead of the considerate, warm hearted Judy that's become the center of my fantasies?* All is saved when Will comes up with the idea of using the tanks from the freezing unit to freeze the plants at their habitable limit, which is forty-four degrees. **What was everyone so worried about? Okay, we had to find Judy. But, who was ever hurt by a flower unless you were allergic to it?** Judy has been rescued, once again, by her brilliant little brother. Now everyone can relax for awhile or at least until a tall, good looking man shows up who is tagged with the name, The Keeper.

"The Keeper"

This episode could become a fan favorite, partly because of our guest star, Michael Rennie. Michael starred in the classic science fiction film *The Day The Earth Stood Still* and is fondly remembered for that movie. Jonathan Harris co-starred with him in the television series, *The Third Man*.

During a work project, **which is anathema to Smith**, he is seized by a mental force that leads him to a specimen cage. He enters it. **If Smith is around, can Will be far behind?** Will watches from behind a boulder as a scary horned monster arrives. The Keeper materializes and subdues the creature with his staff and leads it to an empty cage, which then vanishes.

Will brings John and Don to where Smith was captured, and they free him. The Keeper resents this meddling and comes to the campsite with his cosmic powered staff, explaining his caging of interesting specimens. He sees humans as primitive. *He must have Smith in mind, but he's looking at Judy and me very thoughtfully.* The Keeper offers Don and Judy the opportunity to become highly valued trophies. *"No thanks, buddy. Cages are for animals and murderers and the only bars I want to see serve cocktails."* They refuse.

Smith secretly wants to take over the Keeper's ship and return to Earth. In fact, he says, "Sometimes violence is necessary." *Thanks for the approval, Zachary. I'll remember that!* The Keeper now casts his attention on Will and Penny. He offers to show them his collection, and when they go with him, he attempts to lure them into his cage. Luckily, they run away. **Whatever happened to the catchphrase, "Do you know where your kids are?" Even in my day, kids caught the devil for being too far from home. Our parents didn't have a magical staff to call us to dinner.** But, the Keeper has a magical staff that is able to call them back to his cages. Smith is also called back when he accidentally knocks the staff out of the Keeper's hand. The kids escape, but Smith sticks around trying to convince the Keeper to travel to Earth and take him along. It doesn't work. The Keeper's not interested.

Back at the spaceship, the robot is guarding the kids. **Now, we know where they are!** The call of the Keeper is heard again, and Will and Penny, after fooling the robot, take off for his ship. **I guess the robot wasn't programmed to be a baby sitter.** Smith is Impervious to the call this time because he uses earplugs. **I wish I had earplugs for every time he screamed when frightened.** Smith is made to lead John and Don to the Keeper's ship. An unholy war breaks out, but the lasers are no match for the Keeper's cosmic powered staff. *God, this is terrible. The lasers are useless. Come on, think of something! The lives of Will and Penny are at stake. I've got it! I just happen to have a slingshot in my back pocket, so if I remember my Eagle Scout training correctly and take good aim, I'll be able to bust his cosmic staff with a stone! Bingo!!* The Keeper loses his power, the kids are freed, and the Keeper decides to take off because of all the trouble. **All is well, but not for long, because Smith is still around, and the adventure will continue with "The Keeper"**

"The Keeper" (Part Two)

Smith, with his robot accomplice at hand, tries to steal the Keeper's spaceship. He screws it up by pushing weird looking globes which frees all the caged animals. John and Don are busy laying some pipes when John tells Don not to look up. *That may be good advice, but I'm going to look anyway. Wish I hadn't! I'm looking at the biggest lizard imaginable with a tongue that would make Mick Jagger jealous. I'll back up quietly while I'm staring at this mammoth monster. Just don't*

trip, Donnie boy. What's John up to? Nice try, John, but throwing a pipe at that lizard is like throwing a toothpick at the Incredible Hulk. "Let's get the heck out of here!" The enormous lizard chases them back to the spaceship when the Keeper materializes and keeps the lizard at bay. He then addresses the group. He is furious with John and Don for the release of his animals. *I can only guess what Smith must be thinking right now,: "Don't look at me, keeper of miscreant creatures." But, Smith has to be at the bottom of this.* The Keeper tells of the great danger the family is in and that he will recall the animals with his staff if Will and Penny are turned over to him, a request that John and Maureen refuse. The Keeper has his own lie detector test. He holds Maureen's hand and looks into her eyes. He can then tell that she is innocent of any wrong doing. Smith refuses to hold his hand, but his guilt is transferred to the Keeper's pulsating belt. Now caught, Smith lies about how some mistake must have released all the animals. *Sure, Smith, it's always a mistake when you cause us problems! I only hope the lizard slurps you up with his tongue and swallows you like an oyster!* Now the Keeper insists that he gets to detain Will and Penny or else the animals will remain free to be a dangerous threat to the remaining Robinsons. Judy mentions to Don the possibility of her and Don taking the place of Will and Penny in the Keeper's scheme. *"That sounds like a good idea, Judy, but it only sounds like one. I'm not sure that it actually is a good idea. What if he puts us in different cages? What if Smith negotiates his way onto the Keeper's ship and has complete control over us? Gosh, you're pretty, Judy. I'll do it!"*

They go to the Keeper's ship. John and Maureen had the same thought and offer themselves as substitutes for their children. The Keeper isn't interested. As John leaves, he throws the Keeper's staff to the ground, breaking it. Once its power is drained, the Keeper is attacked by his most sinister specimen. Escaping a choke hold, he falls to the ground unconscious. **"What goes around, comes around," as the great philosopher, Charlie Brown, once said.** Meanwhile, Smith and the kids are on their way to see the Keeper. And double meanwhile, John, Don Maureen, and Judy separate and set out in search of the missing children. Don and Judy take the Chariot which is a good thing because, after finding the kids and Smith, they are attacked by a giant spider who rocks and rolls the Chariot side to side. Don tries his best to get the Chariot to move. *"Damn. It ran a little while ago. Come on you poor excuse for a trolly car! Close the hatch, Will! The spider is getting his hairy leg into the Chariot. Smith, stop screaming and hit that hairy thing. Use your fist! Use your arm! Use anything. Just get it the hell out of here!!"* Something is holding us back.We're being engulfed by something I used to step on as a kid! I can feel the heat of a laser. Will is with us, so it must be John who is firing his laser at this ugly spider.

Triple meanwhile, Maureen helps the Keeper regain consciousness and with his staff which now works (I guess the cosmic staff has a mind of its

own), they exit the ship. **Double triple meanwhile, John's laser isn't effective against the gigantic spider and the Chariot, with its occupants, seems doomed.** *The spider is moving away. I can see the beam of the Keeper's cosmic staff. We're safe!*

The keeper has his caged monsters gathered now and leaves in peace. **As a gesture of remembrance, he leaves the most dangerous of all monsters to the family Robinson and their pilot, Don West. The monster is an angry, caged Zachary Smith who says repeatedly, "Let me out of here. Do you here me? Let me out of here!" Looks like he'll have to wait for the sky pirate to arrive before being free to cause mischief again.**

"The Sky Pirate"

The opening of this show is part of the *John and Don Show*. Remember? They are locked in a space capsule. Now that they are out of the way, the writer of this episode can concentrate on the sky pirate dealing with Will, Smith and the robot.

Smith first encounters the pirate, A.P. Tucker, out in the desert, but then Will is captured because of the pirate's teleporting mechanical parrot. The pirate commands them to take him to the Jupiter 2, where Smith orders the robot to attack the invader. Alas! The mechanical parrot snatches the power pack from the robot who is nothing without it. This allows the sky pirate to use Will as a hostage to get food from the spaceship.

Over a short period of time, Tucker enchants Will with his pirate stories and wins his trust. He even joins Will in saying his bedtime prayers. **That's sweet, but would Maureen consent to such an arrangement? We know where John and Don are during this time but where are the ladies of the Jupiter 2? If they were there, would they have let the sky pirate take Will to his hideout, a cave in the desert? Even though Tucker likes Will's company, he plans on using him as a bargaining chip.**

Tucker then visits the Jupiter 2 and says he will return Will in exchange for repairs to his spaceship. **Don got pretty feisty with the pirate, moving in on him with threatening gestures. Although, nothing physical came of Don's advances, I wonder what was going on in his hawkish mind.** *Who are you to be coming into our lives and holding one of us as a hostage? Think you're cute or something with your pigtailed mustache, ridiculous outfit and little robotic robin perched on your slumping shoulder?* The pirate insists that he will only return Will Robinson when Don and John repair his ship. **He came to the right planet because if John and Don can't fix his alien ship in their homemade spacecraft repair shop, then it obviously can't be done.**

When Tucker returns to his hideout, he continues his friendship with Will, so much so, that he confides in him that he confiscated a machine from an alien

Galaxy that he has hidden in the cave. It is a special device that projects the future of any particular person. When a weird, alien ship arrives, the sky pirate and Will take off for the hills. In the meantime, John and Don work diligently on the rocket's masterful hyper-drive, which propels the ship to travel at twice the speed of light. *"Why are we working on this phony pirate's ship instead of the Jupiter 2? Okay, to get Will back, I understand that, but I don't trust him, Long John Silver, Captain Hook or any of their peg legged friends." This ship's hyper drive is a lot more simple than what Alpha Control created. I do believe we can fix it.* While the repair continues, Will and Tucker are chased by a huge blob that looks utterly disgusting, but it only wants to take the confiscated projector back to where it belongs. The blob gets it back when it is dropped by the fleeing pirate.

Our heroes finally fix the pirate's spaceship, and one of them was right about the pirate not being able to be trusted. When Captain Tucker tells Will that he really isn't a real pirate after all, Will is disillusioned but bravely takes the news like the trooper he is. And the trooper he is will be needed, because his best buddy, the robot, is soon to be in the war of the robots.

"The War of the Robots"

This is definitely a show where the robot can shine. The episode establishes an intelligent robot who is capable of emotion and thought processes. He becomes a "human" robot. He also takes on Robby the Robot of *Forbidden Planet* fame. Don has his problems giving the robot his due, but I'm sure he would be the first to admit that the robot really comes through in this episode.

This show starts out innocently enough with Will, the robot and Dr. Smith fishing. **I would like to see Smith catch something besides hell from Don.** On their way home, Will discovers an old rusted robotoid. The Robinson robot says it is dangerous. Will dismisses the warning and tells his dad about the discovery. John says the robotoid is worthless but allows Will to see if he can restore it. *Go ahead and fix it Will. The worst scenario is that it ends up killing all of us.*

On the other hand, maybe it was a bakery chef on another planet and could make a Boston Creme pie. I'd like that! I'm concerned, though, that our robot warned us that this robotoid has free will and could be dangerous. "If you think our robot is just reflecting his jealousy, Will, then go ahead and use your ingenuity to bring it to life."

That night, the Robinson robot, convinced it is very dangerous, intends to destroy the already damaged robotoid but is stopped by the conniving Dr. Smith who wants to wait and see if the robotoid could be useful to him. **Smith would keep a crushed worm around if he thought that someday he could use it to his advantage.**

The new robot, although in terrible condition, comes to life through the efforts of Will. *What do you know? He can converse. Thank God, I will have someone new to talk with.* The robotoid says he is a servant and can repair just about anything. *Yes! This is just what I need. A day or two off from fixing the Chariot, the force field, the drilling equipment or anything else that might get broken by Smith or a disgruntled alien. I feel happy for the first time since that oily, musky smelling A.P. Tucker went yonder into the black void of the universe. I can't wait! A few days off from work, work, work. But what will I do? Chess bores me. I mastered that when I was four years old. I like to cook but Maureen won't let me near the kitchen. Will won't let me touch his guitar and I hate Penny's taste in music, so what the hell will I do? Hmm, no chance of that! John Robinson put a chastity belt on his daughter that reaches from Earth to Alpha Centauri.*

All I've left to do is worry, worry, worry. Worry about Smith. Worry about aliens that come out of the woodwork. Worry about the precarious nature of this environment. Okay, relax. Everything works out, so just take one day at a time.

The robotoid sneaks off and contacts his leader. He is told that the Robinsons are needed for experimentation and to capture them. Back at the Jupiter, he repairs the Chariot. **It is always in need of repair.** *One less worry for me!* The Robinson robot takes off for the desert **Where else? Fenway Park?** after he is embarrassingly made to feel worthless by the robotoid and insulted by Dr. Smith. *If I have to choose between robots right now, I'll go with the new one.* That night, Will treks off to find his best friend. The robot tells him that the new robot is wicked and sends Will back to the Jupiter 2. The next morning, the family wakes up to missing lasers, a destroyed force field generator and a disabled Chariot. **Good choice, Don. Now, you have something to worry about. Happy?**

The family is gathered together in one place so that the alien leader can use them for his own evil purpose. Luckily, Will breaks free and finds the robot. *There goes that kid, again. Making me look bad, so I guess I have to stay back with the family and worry, worry, worry.* When Will and the robot return to the Jupiter 2 campsite, they come up with a plan to drain the robotoid's power in a battle between the robots and to end the robotoid's dominance forever.

All ends happily with a new relationship between the robot and the Robinson family based on trust and love. **Thanks, Will for saving the day and proving that Don's judgement isn't always correct. But, we can't blame him for making some bad choices. It's not as if he were always ready to take the challenge.**

"The Challenge"

This episode is one our better shows. Written by Barney Slater and directed by Don Richardson, it stars two really terrific actors, Michael Ansara and Kurt Russell.

A young boy on a survival mission shows up at the Jupiter 2 campsite. The mission was instigated by his father, the ruler in another world. The boy carries only a spear. *If I had a son and it doesn't look like that will ever happen, I sure as heck wouldn't send him out after dark on this planet with only a spear as protection. He's good looking with an athletic build and speaks intelligently, but he seems to be sneering at the women.* He says that in his world women know their place. *"Whoa there, young man, are you telling us that you live in a place where there are no women's rights? You mean to tell me that here in space there are worlds that resemble Earth back before the feminist movement? I'm sorry, Maureen. I don't mean to be disrespectful, but it's kind of remarkable to think that a "man's world" still exists somewhere. What's that, Judy? What do I mean by "a man's world"? Just, I guess, a world where people get along and "know their place." No, I don't mean for you to "know your place," so to speak. "So to speak" is just an expression, Maureen. Yes, I am committed to women's rights. I just think that it is important that women also "know their place", so to speak." Wow, why did I let myself get into that exchange? I'm such a jerk when I let a little bit of my bias toward men's rights get in the way of my political correctness.*

The boy's name is Quano, and he answers only his father. He thinks Will is a coward when Will won't fight him. **That is a circumstance in which no boy or man wants to find himself.** He takes Will to a cave where a monster lives to prove his survival instincts. **Now, there's a cave that John and Don somehow missed. That and the Batcave.** Quano trips while challenging the beast and is caught off guard. Will comes to his aid, just before Quano's father shows up to drive off the beast. **Good timing dad, but I suspect you were keeping tabs on your son in case the beast was too much of a challenge for Quano.** The boy's father admires the courage of Will, and they head back to the Jupiter. There, the ruler meets Smith and the soft, flaccid handshake of the doctor leaves him in disbelief at this supposed specimen of manhood. **I'm sure Smith gave his best shot at a strong handshake, but his limp wrist got in the way.** Quano is a bully and his taunts toward Will lead to a scuffle and to Will accepting a challenge from Quano. Maureen,however, disapproves. **Now the male-female controversy really takes hold and, surprisingly enough, Maureen's wishes yield to John's throughout the coming contest. In fact, when Maureen says something very wise about the upcoming competition and Penny asks her to explain her remark, she even tells Penny to ask her dad, instead.**

Smith **(he's everywhere)** overhears the ruler telling Quano that if he loses, all witnesses will be destroyed to hide the shame. Smith then overtrains Will so he will be tired and lose. The challenge ends in a tie, and the fathers take over the contest with high voltage swords. **Little did the ruler know that swordsmanship is a talent of Professor Robinson. He never heard of Zorro on his planet.** It is a good match with sparks flying everywhere. John Robinson wins, and sportsmanship triumphs. The ruler concedes, and he and his son are reconciled as they go in search of the cave monster. **Feminism will have to be dealt with later because I have a feeling that the male remains the dominant sex on the ruler's planet. But wait a minute, feminism can be dealt with immediately because the colonists are on their way.**

"The Colonists"

The family is setting up three radio stations in remote areas to make communications better. **This is strange when you consider that they only need to communicate with each other, but sometimes they pick up weird sound waves from other weird aliens like themselves. And now they do it again.** The family picks up an alien sound wave that destroys their receivers. Then, for some unknown reason, Judy and Penny vanish. **Why? Are there any apparent**

reasons in space? In a different location, Don and Smith get a signal that Judy and Penny are being kept prisoners. Then again, for no apparent reason, Don's laser explodes. *"I don't know how you pulled this one off, Smith, but what the hell have you done? And don't give me that innocent puppy dog look when it's done something wrong. Whose voice is that ordering us back to the Jupiter 2? We had better find out, so drag your lazy body back to the ship."*

When Don and Smith arrive, they realize that John, Maureen, Will and the robot are also missing. Don and Smith go looking for them. **Where would you look? The same place they did. In a cave. Hide and seek would be a fun game to play on this planet except there would only be one place to hide and that's in one of the countless caves. No one would ever be found. The name of the game would be hide and die.** Don and Smith are captured and taken by Amazon warriors before their leader, Noble Niolani. **Here is where fanatical feminism raises its ugly head. She despises men!** Noble Niolani explains that the planet is being colonized by warrior women. *Besides being ridiculed, mocked and scoffed at, this is kind of intriguing. The warriors are shapely, fairly pretty and walk like they are on a walkway in a fashion show. Niolani is rather beautiful in her black sequenced leotard but her headdress leaves a lot to be desired. It looks like an underwater bomb from World War ll with spikes protruding from all sides.*

Oh, oh. We were just told that we were going to be used to clear the grounds and build a construct like the

MacDonald's hamburger arch. Smith just started drooling until he heard the arch will be used to purify the air so the new colonists will be able to breath the air on the new planet. Maureen is placed with Judy and Penny who are being brainwashed to dislike men. Penny is learning fast and shows off her new status on Will. It takes Judy longer to come around. **It must be Don's positive male influence on her.**

Now, If Noble Niolani thinks she is making a slave out of me, she has another think coming, because I have a good idea of how John and I can escape even though we are being imprisoned by a force field. **It wasn't a good enough idea, Don. You were caught in seventeen seconds.** *Okay, we'll try again, later.* **Good try, Don. You were recaptured in thirty-one seconds.** *This is getting demoralizing, but wait, Maureen is turning off the force field. Good going, Maureen! Now, we're really out of here!* **Sure you are!** John and Don are recaptured yet again. **You're getting closer to escape, Don. You are quite amazing! This time it took you forty-seven seconds to get captured. At this rate, old buddy, you'll be free in about three million seconds of trying over a ten year period.** *To borrow a phrase of Dr. Smith's that I can't stand but will use, "Oh, the pain." I don't want to be a slave even for ten seconds. Especially to gorgeous women who think I'm a twerp. Or even worse, think I'm a man. Where the heck is Will when you need him, which is always?* In the interim, Will and Smith escape, go to the drill site, take some explosives and blow up the arch. *You are the man, Will! You are my* *hero, forever!* This makes the planet unsuitable for the warriors to live on and they return to No Man's Land. *I swear that I will do my best to never crash land there.* **With some good luck, Don, maybe some day you'll crash land near a pretty gal who won't enslave you, especially if she is one of the space croppers.**

"The Space Croppers"

This show reads like one of the better shows during our first year. Great guest stars are lined up, and the dialogue is very good. The story is quirky, but it works on a certain level. What that level is, when it comes to way out science fiction, is anybody's guess. This is our twenty-fifth show of our first year, and I suspect a trend to feature Dr. Smith is beginning to happen. Out of our first twenty-four shows, fourteen featured the entire cast. Three others were about Will, and two were about Penny. John, Judy and the robot each appeared prominently in one show. Episodes twenty-three, twenty-four and twenty-five were completely about Smith. Maybe I missed something, but not one show was devoted to Maureen or my alter-ego, Don West. I think that if they hook up Smith with the robot and Will, the show, in its second year, will become about their adventures and less about the family's problems. Don? His fate seems to hinge on the irritated relationship that he has developed with Dr. Smith.

Will, Penny and Dr. Smith are working on a time capsule **(that's one way to keep the kids preoccupied)**, when they hear the howl of a wolf. Smith is sure it is a werewolf. He's right. On their way back to the campsite, a werewolf appears, who later turns into a mute hillbilly named Keel, who takes them to his spaceship which is a log cabin with jets. **The ship is really a stereotypical habitat of a Hatfield or McCoy. They even have an outhouse where they grow treacherous flowers. But more flirtatious than treacherous is Effra the sister of the mute hillbilly. The Daisy Mae of this episode, played to the hilt by Sherry Jackson, shows up ready to sexually provoke any male in sight. Right now it is Will and Smith, but can Don be far behind? Her mother, Sybilla, who acts and looks like she eats shredded concrete with her cheerios, throws them all out.**

Keel and Effra visit the Jupiter to borrow some sort of seasoning for their plants. Effra comes on to Don. *Give me strength, Lord, to resist this enticing temptress. I wish you wouldn't touch my face like that. Darn, I knew I should have shaved this morning. Now, she's running her finger down the zipper of my velour shirt. Darn, I knew I should have showered this morning. You sure are pretty* and sexy. *"I'm kind of involved...Ya know?"* And she's just shown up. *I don't know why you're chuckling, Judy. Am I blushing?* Keel and Effra leave without incident.

That night, weird sounds of ceremonial singing are heard by the family. We all donned **(or is it Johnned?)** our bathrobes to come outside to listen. *"That's Voo-doo alright. It's straight out of The Beatles last album. Sorry, Penny, I couldn't help the comparison. Okay, let's get dressed and go see."*

John, Maureen, Don and Smith leave the ship to look into it. The hillbilly aliens are spewing some kind of magical witchcraft to make their plants grow. *I'll be darned, sorcery in space. We meet the best people up here. I can't wait to tell my kids (if I'm ever lucky enough to have any) about the musical trio of Sybilla, Keel and Effra. Add Smith to the group, and they can be called "The Rolling Groans."* Sybilla tells them to get lost! **(Didn't she know that we were already lost?)**

Smith can't take a hint so he returns the next day. The plants have grown, and the hillbillies have gotten all dressed up, fancy like, for another magical ceremony. With a plan to get back to Earth using their space craft, Smith woos Sybilla. Meanwhile, Effra tries to seduce Don, but his Boy Scout loyalty wins out. She then wants to bewitch him and asks Will to cut off a lock of his curly hair. Will doesn't do it. **Thank God nothing comes of this because Don without his helmet of black hair is like Michael Jackson without his white glove.** In the meantime, John has discovered that the plants are deadly. With the harvest in, the hillbillies plan to leave. Smith thinks he will be leaving with them because of his proposal to marry Sybilla. Will tries to warn Smith off but is attacked by the werewolf and knocked into a full grown plant. Effra helps Will out but then drops him back into the plant when he doesn't produce Don's curly lock. **(Can you imagine what that curly lock would go for on E-Bay?)** The family then arrive and destroys the plants with spray cans of Raid. Smith comes to realize that the hillbilly family is far too cultish for him and he, Don and the Robinsons bid farewell to the mojo clan. **I'm sure they joined the lost civilization.**

"The Lost Civilization"

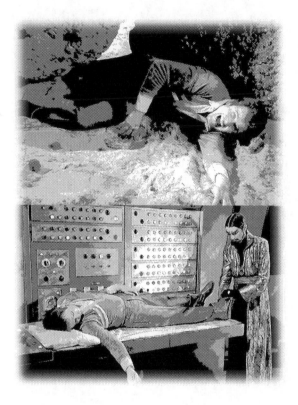

This episode has the very best location shots of the Chariot traveling over the rocky terrain and vast desert of Red Rock Canyon State Park in Cantil, California. Although shot in black and white, the various screenshots are really impressive. Don West has quite a bit to do in this episode, so let's find out how he handled it. After all, I did mention earlier that he never had a show that featured him. Here's

his chance to sink or swim. Or, as it turns out, to limp or walk.

John, Will, Don and the robot are out searching for drinking water. The Chariot's air conditioner is broken, and the temperature is 110 and rising. **The sweat on Don's face almost looks like real.** *"Boy, these velour shirts are hot! Are you sure, John, that it would be inappropriate to go shirtless? The girls aren't around. No, huh? Well, we better find a cave soon for shaded shelter, or we'll end up like dark russet potato chips."*

Finding a cave **(they are everywhere)**, John and Don fix the air conditioner. Will unhappily spills the beans on Smith who replaced a part for his own selfish use. *I can't believe that I'm under the Chariot fixing this stupid air conditioner while Smith is back in his air-conditioned room, cool and relaxed, thinking about what it might have been like to have been married to Sybilla. I wish he had gone off to LaLa land and married her. I wonder who would get first pick of the litter if they had kids? I can't fix this blasted thing! My kingdom for a drink of water. Okay, then a lock of my hair for a drink of water. I'm getting delirious. Wait!! "John, I got it working!"*

While they were working, Will and the robot went exploring. This wasn't a very good idea since they both fell into a sinkhole. It turns out that they unexpectedly discovered an underground lake and forest area. ***That's good because they were looking for water but bad because now they don't know where Will has gone***. *"Can't anybody stay in one place for more than a minute? Kids get antsy? That's your answer,*

John? Now, we have to go find them, so let's get with it." While searching for them, a giant rock falls on Don's ankle. *I'm in pain, but I have to act like a mensch. If John sees that I'm anything less than a warrior, he'll stop taking me on these fun excursions. God, my foot hurts!* "John, do something! What do you mean the boulder is too big to move? Get a limb to use as a lever. You only have to lift it inches to relieve the pressure on my foot. That's it! I'm free." *But the pain is still there. I'll use the limb as a crutch and hop around like a three-legged bunny rabbit, looking for a boy and his friend.* **Little do our heroes know that they are being watched by clones of Ray Walston of** *My Favorite Martian.*

Will and the robot find a princess asleep on a bed in the forest. Alas, Sleeping Beauty. She awakens when Will gives her a kiss. At about this time, John and Don are captured by soldiers who are dressed in Roman gladiator skirts. *Cute outfits but I'm not fooling with those guys. They were probably rejects from Niolani's amazon warrior colonists. Up here in space who knows what anyone's sex is anymore. At least Earthlings know what they are and why they are what they are. Most of them, anyway.*

The princess takes Will to Major Domo who in turn takes him to where his father and Don are kept prisoners. He first miraculously cures Don's sprained ankle and then explains that his army is going to attack Earth when the time is right. **I wonder if Major Domo outranks Major West? Or outlasts him? We shall see. I know one thing, he sure is good at fixing**

an injured foot. The princess is in charge, so no order is given. She wants to marry Will, but he refuses. **Of all the excuses, he tells her he wants to have fun! Fun? Doesn't he realize that marriage is fun? Ask any married man if he's having fun, and he'll laugh at you like a fool for asking such a foolish question.** Will remains with Major Domo. Realizing she can't marry Will, the princess frees John who is handcuffed to a wall. During an ensuing earthquake, John, Will and the robot release Don from his shackles.

Major Domo is killed when he falls into some machinery and is electrocuted. **I guess Major West wins.** The princess goes back to sleep, after declining an invitation to go with our foursome who head back home in their air-conditioned chariot. *I hope we pass a Seven-Eleven on our way back because we didn't take the water when we had the chance, and I am really dying for a good old Moxie.* **But things are looking up, Major West, because soon there will be a change of space.**

"A Change of Space"

This script had me chuckling because of the premise. A time machine is discovered which makes Will brilliant (wasn't he always?) and Dr. Smith old (wasn't he always?) so, let's see what they're up to.

Climbing a plateau, Will and Smith spot some glimmering lights. **No, Zachary, it's not Las Vegas. But, I bet you wish it were so you could finagle millions from the casino owners and turn rich gamblers into homeless hobos, being the deceiver that you are.** The lights turn out to be a craft sitting on some power machinery. Will and Smith encounter pits of cosmic dust as they walk to investigate the source. Smith falls into a pit, but Will, as usual, pulls him out.

The entire crew tramps out to see what the craft is. The robot analyzes it as a space relay station. *Why the heck did we all come out here when only the robot was needed? Come to think of it, he did give us some unbelievable information.* The craft can travel at the speed of light squared and crosses the fifth dimension. *There's that stupid fifth dimension, again. I thought we already went through that. And I wonder what Albert Einstein would say about traveling at the speed of light squared. He probably would think you'd have to be lost in space to believe that one!*

John orders the relay station off limits, and as everyone begins to leave the robot is disabled by an undetected cosmic ray. *Where did that ray come from? I'm glad it was directed toward the robot, because I sure as heck don't want to be put out of commission.* John saying that the space relay station is off limits is all that Will needs to go back that evening to fix the robot. The problem occurs when Will's curiosity gets the better of him to explore the craft, and the vehicle takes off with him aboard. The robot tells the family members who immediately go back to the relay station. *"What'd you expect, John? You told him it was off limits! Must be great to have a son who listens so well. Yeah, okay, he went to fix the robot. I know he means well, but he gets himself in the most difficult situations. Yes, Maureen, I know it's not his fault entirely, but he's too smart not to realize there are consequences to being too curious. No, Judy, I'm not picking on your brother, but here comes the space vehicle now!"* The spaceship returns and Will disembarks looking like he normally does. That's deceptive, though, since we can't see into his mind which has been increased by brilliance squared. Gradually, however, this becomes apparent when his behavior turns rude and arrogant and he alienates the family.

But not Smith. He wants some of that intelligence. **I guess the ship is still off limits, but who would have known?** Will shows Smith how to operate the vehicle and Smith takes off. When he returns, he is no smarter but has aged considerably. He looks about one hundred years old. He has a long white beard, wears a shawl and is seated in a 1930s wheelchair. *Wow, look at that old crotchety geezer! I want to laugh but that would be cruel. I think I'll be half cruel and smile broadly but so that no one will see me.* John and Don try to figure out a way to make Smith younger but can't come up with anything. **I don't think Don was really putting his mind to the task, but he does show some compassion by offering Smith some hot soup.** *I wish I could stop hoping he might burn his tongue while sipping Maureen's space broth. Show some caring. Don't be such a hard-ass. Maybe aging will change his evil, devious, deceitful, dishonest, unscrupulous, unethical, unprincipled and underhanded ways. Maybe, but not likely.* Will, now brilliant as he is, has the idea of reversing the process by taking another trip and leaves with Dr. Smith. **You'd think this was Disneyland with all the rides that are going on.** John is furious once again and the family treks out to the landing spot. *Well, I'm glad someone else is as pissed off as I am about Will's behavior.* Another ship unexpectedly lands and an amphibious lizard-like alien gets out. *"Is that you, Will? Your eyes are all buggy and you're all scaly. You don't look so good, Will."* The alien points his finger, and a laser beam knocks Don's pistol from his hand. *That's not fair, lizard-man. Finger control should be a law on this planet.* Next, Will's ship lands, and he is back to his normal self. Smith then makes the trip, and he returns normal. **(whatever his "normal" may be).** The alien decides to leave. **And who could blame him after dealing with a young man and an old man who are obsessed with taking rides in his space vehicle? But joy rides are not the crimes that make the The Robinson family, Smith and Don West the prisoners of space.**

"The Prisoners of Space"

In this episode, It looks like the scales of justice are about to become a major concern to the Robinsons and Don West. If justice is to be served in outer space, how will it be apportioned evenly?

Smith is becoming a wine maker. **But, where the heck did the grapes come from? The hydroponic garden? I think not.** While Will and the robot look on, a creature with one eye hanging from its forehead and carrying a machine scares the hell out of them. **Why is it that there**

are so many one-eyed monsters in space? Could it be that they evolved over millions of years from zeroing in on too many computer games? The creature follows them to the Jupiter 2. It puts the machine on a rock, and it contacts the family. It delivers a message from the Galaxy Tribunal of Justice and is indicts everyone except Dr. Smith. *Well, this looks like fun. A day in court! I'm sure they got me for reckless driving but why everyone else? And why not Smith? I hope this doesn't end up being a kangaroo court, or we're all doomed. Don't panic. Just tell the truth, the whole truth and nothing but the truth. Oh, now I see why Smith isn't going to be summoned. His tenet would be, "Just tell a lie, another lie and nothing but a lie."*

The Robinson family and Don are fenced in by a force field until they are transported to an alien world and called before the judge. John is summoned before the court which is made up of weird looking aliens. Sitting in a chair, two devices activate his brain, and John's memory of the Jupiter launch comes up on a screen. **I hope when Don is called his racy memories when he was on earth are wiped from his mind.** John is cleared. Don is next to sit in the chair and is given the solar wrench that John lost while working on Jupiter's scanner. Littering is a serious offense. *Are you kidding me? A lousy little solar wrench in billions of square miles is going to mess up the atmosphere? You aliens are worse than the EPA.* Don gets angry and tries to cover for John. He is told to be quiet and then he is released. Will is up next and is in trouble for waking up a bubble creature when he entered the ship, the Derelict.

(The bubble creature was probably a government worker.)

It is a surprise for Smith when he is told he will be called as a witness. He panics because his lies may become transparent. He plots an escape with the help of Will and the robot. With the protection of darkness, the three amigos dig a hole under the force field fence. The next day Will confesses, and the tribunal gives permission to Will and the robot to look for Smith. They find him, and he agrees to return and face the music.

Now, all this is happening while John, Don and the women are doing what? We did bring along a lot of board games and we are, after all, prisoners in our own spaceship. So, I guess we were all down on the first deck, in the kitchen, playing Space Monopoly. It's more fun without Smith, seeing that he always cheats. But, he couldn't cheat the tribunal.

Dr. Smith's memory about his sabotaging our mission is recalled, and he is found guilty. He is under spaceship arrest, but John gets him released on an insanity plea. *"My God, John, a petition, attesting to Smith's craziness, is what you want me to sign? Alright, he belongs in Loony Tunes, and we have a chance to get rid of him in a lawful manner. The evidence has been seen by a judge and jury. So what if they're monsters! Judy, stop treating me like I'm the monster and ease up on the chokehold. I'll sign, I'll sign".* God, she's strong for a Barbie doll look alike. Smith doesn't like the idea but goes along with it. The Tribunal also goes along with this arrangement, and the charge is dismissed. **I imagine Dr. Smith considers a free insane Smith is better than an imprisoned sane Smith if he's to get ready for a wild adventure.**

"Wild Adventure"

The Robinson family is back in space when Smith decides to toy with the astrogator. He becomes excited because he is able to get a fix on the planet Earth. *"We're not going to Earth, Dum-Dum, so get the heck away from the astrogator!"* Smith won't let go of the astrogator handle, and he and the Major both grab it and struggle. When the handle pulls out of the unit, the ship bucks and swerves and all hell breaks loose.

Everybody to the left, then everybody to the right as Irwin bangs the tin film can . As the special effects crew set off the firecrackers and cause smoke to bellow from the base of the astrogator, Don looks for the fire extinguisher. *What was that handle made of? How could it come out so easily? Get the extinguisher quick,* *and put out the flames! Good!! That's done, and there's the handle of the astrogator on the floor. Now, get it back in the unit! It fits. Just like a plug in an old fashioned bath tub. That was easy.* The ship comes back under control. *Now for Smith!* "You can't back away from me, Smith. I'm going to rip you into little pieces and let them float away in space one by one." Smith shows Don the piece of paper that is marked with the Jupiter's present position in the star system. Don advances on Smith but stops when Smith threatens to swallow the paper. *Maybe I can help him swallow it with a karate chop to the throat.*

John makes a deal with Smith, who is very happy, thinking we are on our way to Earth. But, he's wrong and at dinner which looks like plastic wrapped jelly beans, Don tells him that going to Earth, is out of the question. *"You see, Smith, because the sun is directly between us and Earth, we would be burnt to a crisp." I can see his feeble mind thinking that we could fly at night or some such nonsense.* He refuses to go to Alpha Centauri. **And to that, Don answers,** *"Smith, anytime you want, I'll be glad to stop the Jupiter and let you off."* Smith leaves the dinner table in a huff and goes to the upper deck.

Angry and petulant, Smith starts pushing buttons to reset the course away from Alpha Centauri and, by accident, releases all the reserve fuel cells. Once again, John and Don are beside themselves but Smith is saved from the wrath of Don when John is able to locate by map a fuel barge a short distance away. **Thank you Alpha Control for positioning the barge at this location. How convenient! That is the kind of**

valuable predictive thinking that is so essential to a successful mission. I'm sure Don agrees. *What luck! Somebody down there guessed right for a change.*

Don gets to walk in space in order to refuel the Jupiter. His chance to be a smidgen of a hero. After getting dressed for the space walk, Don enters the air lock. *Okay, so far so good. The helmut fits good and snug, but it is fogging up a little. Push this button, and the outdoor airlock should open. Good. Now, attach the tether hook with the screw eye bolt. That should be easy. Hmm, not so easy. These damn gloves are too big and clumsy. The screw eye is too little and my plastic visor is steaming up again. I should have asked for the gold coated visor, but I thought I would save Alpha Control some money. Big deal! A thirty billion dollar operation, and I wanted to save them $29.95! Got it. The tether is hooked. Let's take a look at the barge's fuel gauge. Nice and easy, now. Just keep holding onto something. Here we are. What the heck...the gage says the supply is half full. Or half empty if you're a pessimist. I had better get back in. What's that I'm looking at? "Who's there?" I'm seeing things. I need some rest!*

It's okay, Don. What you saw was a green skinned girl, who is one of the People of the Green Mist. You don't need rest. You need a psychiatrist. But, put that on hold until you get the whole story.

Her name is Athena, and she feeds off of atomic fuel. Her language is a mathematical progression, and she is in love with Dr. Smith, as she so lovingly sing-songs to him. **Need a psychiatrist, yet? There's no time. You see, Smith tricked Penny into resetting**

the controls for Earth. The danger signal sounds, and the ship is on a path that will take it to the sun. *"John, we have to set a new course! We're heading straight for the sun! What? We can reset a course for Earth? Let's do it!* "The green lady returns, however, and hypnotizes Smith so he decides to join her. **How he got past our heroes, got dressed in a space suit and went for a walk with his new girlfriend, Athena, is beyond me, and I don't expect Don to try to figure it out or his mental breakdown will be imminent . We can't have that because he has to go out in space after Smith.**

"What do you mean, I have to go after Smith? We're set to go back to Earth now. We can't do both. We can't make the course correction and get him. I say, let him float. He's in good company. An atomic fuel drinking, green lady who can't sing is the perfect companion for him. Why are you all looking at me like that? I can't believe I'm doing this, but I swear on my boy scout honor this is the last and only time I'll save his ... . Never mind, help me get my gear on."

But, what good did it do for Don to save Smith when he could so easily become one of the condemned of space.

"Condemned of Space"

Finally, we are into our third season. I love the intros and music but I'm not crazy about our new costumes. I imagine the stories can only get better after the cartoony and overly campy episodes of the second season. I found the first show to be pretty interesting, measuring up in a way that more approximates science fiction. Those are my feelings, but let's see what our space hero thinks of the first show of our third season.

The robot sounds an alarm **(what else)**. A comet is approaching **(what else)** and is heading right for us **(what else).** We are prepared to leave **(what else)** and take off just in time **(what else)** to avoid a collision with a fiery comet. Dressed in their sparkling silver lame pajamas, John and Don are anxiously getting ready to get the Jupiter in the air. *"What's that, John? Emergency lift off procedures?" "Got it!" Damned if I can remember the difference between regular and emergency procedures. The top green button is for go, I know that, and the green one below that it is for go-go, which, I guess, would give the ship more power in an emergency. Or is it the other way around? Crap, I feel as stupid as Smith. "I am hurrying, John. What? Full forward thrust?" I don't do so well under this kind of pressure, John, so stop barking at me with all these commands. Hell, I'll push all the buttons. That's what Smith would do. It's working! we're taking off!! "I think we made it!!!" I can't believe we did. Boy, Alpha Control really needs some different colored buttons for the lift off procedures.*

The Robinsons dodged the comet by flying over it. *That is the best flying I've done since I landed a paper airplane on Betsy Noble's desk in the second grade. But it looks like I might have to do some more fancy flying; because there is a supernova approaching from the right of us, and everyone is transfixed on it.* **A supernova is a stellar explosion that briefly outshines an entire galaxy, radiating as much energy as the sun is expected to emit over its entire life span before fading from view.** *Holy Moses! A Supernova! Evading that comet was*

like evading a rowboat compared to evading the Titanic.
"What's that Smith, we're doomed?" A fairly accurate choice
of a word, Smith. But we have a little time before doomsday.
That should be Smith's middle name. Zachary Doomsday
Smith. Sounds about right.

As John and Don work on the controls, Smith
accidentally sends the robot out into space. **He doesn't**
push the colored buttons any better than Don, but
his results are always catastrophic. Now John has
to go out and get The robot. He gets a "Good Luck,
John." from Maureen. *That'll help a lot, Maureen. That*
and my getting this ship into retro thrust, which I can't
manage to do. Maybe if I had a rabbit's foot I could get lucky
but, then again, it wasn't very lucky for the rabbit. Oh, well,
John didn't have much luck either and is returning to the
ship. I'm sure that when Maureen said "John, come in now",
he didn't have much of a choice but to listen.

With the successful rescue effort over, the Jupiter
2 is now being sucked into the supernova. **That**
sounds bad, but it is actually good because within
the supernova there is an alien spaceship on which
the crew can dock. The robot is sucked in also, so he's
safe as well. The lower part of the Jupiter locks into the
upper part of the alien space station, so John and Don
go below to find someone to ask for spare parts. *"This*
is worse than going to Walmart's. No one's around!" Don
and John look through a frosted pane of glass on a
door that reveals frozen men on pedestals. *"Wow, these*
guys look pretty cool! What's that? I'm not wisecracking,
John, I'm just trying to be cool, myself" They enter the

room where about eight or nine men dressed in grey monastery-like outfits are in different threatening poses with knives and machetes. *Boy, are these guys ugly and tough looking! I sure as hell wouldn't want to date one of their sisters!* John realizes that this station must be a prison. There's a broken clock, and there are dials on the bases of the pedestals the inmates are perched on. John pushes a dial over to the red side, and it frees one of the convicts. An alarm goes off. *"Good move, John. This isn't chess, ya know." This ugly convict is trying to give me a haircut with his machete. "I'm getting the hell out of here!"*

A prison robot with a stun rifle shows up and puts the inmate back on his pedestal. *That's a weird looking robot. Big fat legs with a domed head makes him menacing. I'll take our cute roly-poly as a companion any day.* The prison robot leads them to a control room where they find the parts they were hoping to locate.

Meanwhile, on the Jupiter, the robot tells Will and Smith that there is another robot below, and there are over nine thousand prisoners being held as inmates. Will and Smith investigate **(which means how can they find and cause trouble for Don).** Smith frees one of the inmates **(who has the poetic name of Phanzig)** and the alarm goes off again. The prison robot grabs Don, thinking he is the escaped prisoner and freezes him. **This really is the pits for Don, being dragged around like a frozen slab of beef. Poor guy has to keep his eyes wide open while being handcuffed to a wall in the control room. Our pilot defrosts** beautifully and denies that he is Phanzig when he is Accused by the head computer. Don is really pissed. You can tell by how his clenched teeth are making his jaw muscles pop out like Arnold Swartzenegger's bi-ceps. *Where's John? Where's the robot? Where's Will? Judy, Maureen, Penny, the bloop? Where's anyone? "I'm not who you think I am! I am who I think I am! Don West! Pilot extraordinaire of the Jupiter 2!! Ask anyone! Even Smith. No!! Don't ask Smith. He lies and doesn't like me." I'm tired, and I want to go home.* Which is what happens when John fixes the broken clock and all the prisoners get to go home. Nice ending. I like it. But not as much as I enjoyed our visit to a hostile planet.

"A Visit to a Hostile Planet"

How about this script? The Robinsons are heading home! Wow!! Who would have ever thought? I'm pretty excited about doing this show. Wait a minute. It takes place on Earth in the year 1947? There's a time warp involved? Really? Well, let's see what happens.

Once away from the prison space station, the Jupiter 2 continues its journey until a problem with the fuel system arises and, while testing it, the power locks in. *"John, the thrust is building. So what? We're about to exceed the speed of light! Are you sure you want maximum thrust? Okay, you're the pilot's boss."* Hold the go-go button down for one minute. This is crazy. *Runaway acceleration is considered radiation speed.*

Don can hardly get up because of the gravitational pull but makes it to another set of buttons. He pushes another button and the ship goes into hyper-drive. *I'm feeling dizzy.* You're not alone, Don. Everyone has collapsed because you sent the ship through a space-time vortex. When the crew comes around, they are approaching Earth. John prepares the ship for re-entry. Which means changing into our silver lame pajamas. He tries to call Alpha Control, but they don't answer. *"There must be a World Series game on."*

Here, Don gets a chance to show off his expert piloting and safely lands the Jupiter on a parking lot. *Nothing to it. This looks like a parking lot where I learned to drive my dad's Chevy. I remember side swiping three cars trying to parallel park. I'm sure glad the lot is completely empty today, or I would have wiped out about a hundred cars.* Don got a round of applause from the Robinson family when he landed the Jupiter so smoothly. Even Dr. Smith gave him a loving tap on the shoulder. *Thanks Smith. I know this a dream come true for you, but hold your enthusiasm because you might just be facing charges down here.*

For some unknown reason (I suspect script plot), the group pair up and go in different directions to look for people living in the area. Smith, of course, takes Will with him. John and Don (The Laurel and Hardy of *Lost in Space*) search together and Maureen, Penny and Judy (that's a pair plus one) go looking as a threesome. The ladies enter a building with an office that has an old fashioned phone on a desk. **The phone can only be seen in movies from the 1940s.** They try to use it to no avail. John and Don come across an antique car in a garage whose The license plate shows it's registered in Michigan in 1947.

"Nineteen forty-seven? That was the year Jackie Robinson became the first African American to play in the Major Leagues. That's right John. I know my baseball history. By the way, was he any relation to you? You say you inherited his athletic ability and credit him for your fencing expertise?"

They inspect the interior of the old car and discover a dashboard radio. John turns it on, and a news report tells of an alien spaceship that has landed on the parking lot of a sawmill and gives the date of October,1947. *"Well, I'll be damned! For once, we're the aliens. Not so funny, huh, John? Oh my God! It's 1947 here! I was right. Alpha Control was watching the World Series, except there was no Alpha Control then or now...I mean in 1947. And there was no... us. I mean you or me! We're in a time lapse of fifty years earlier than when we left Earth. Boy, oh, boy, I never thought this was possible. I could actually be my own grandpa. Yeah, I'll shut up, John. It's just that I'm excited and confused at the same time."*

Meanwhile, Two hicks from this small town try to arrest Will and Smith in the lumberyard building but are thwarted by zings from the robot. They head back to the Jupiter after being identified as Voltons by the hicks.

Everyone is now back at the ship, trying to figure out what to do next.

Don tells them that the inertia guidance system is damaged, and it will take all night to repair. *I better get this right. I got us into this time warp mess and it's up to me to get us out of it.* Smith wants to stay no matter the year because with his knowledge of the future he thinks he can rule the world. The others want to get back to their normal time.

The next day after Don has repaired the broken system, Judy and Penny get permission from John to go apple picking on a farm nearby. That starts a series of adventures for the "aliens." Judy gets lassoed by a young, good looking farm hand, but John and Don rescue her from this predicament. Will gets caught by the sheriff's deputies and is kept in a barn where he meets a young lady his age who later helps him evade the townsfolk by disguising him as a farm boy and the robot as a farm girl. **I'm glad Don wasn't involved in these scenes with the robot dressed like that, or he might have proposed after losing all sense of reality.** Smith takes the side of the sheriff and the townspeople by acting the part of a fireman and taking charge of an imminent assault on the Jupiter 2 so he can stay on Earth. John tries to calm down the townsfolk but is taken hostage and stripped of his laser rifle. Luckily for Don and the Robinsons, the sheriff's cannon misfires **(you'd think Don was in charge of firing the cannon)**, and in the confusion John recovers his laser rifle. Holding the mob at bay, everyone makes it back to the ship, including Smith who, in a panic, decides he'd rather leave with the Robinsons after all. **Quite a Visit but not as much fun as a visit to Hades.**

"A Visit to Hades"

Really looking forward to filming this episode. It reads funny, and the guest star, Gerald Mohr, is a wonderful actor with whom I worked on *Johnny Ringo*. Also, Don has a fight scene with him that should prove interesting. This episode is comedic, and both Judy and Don get a chance to have some fun for a change come HELL or high water.

Dr. Smith discovers a lyre **(himself?)** and is about to pluck his way into Hades. This lyre or harp is the key to the underworld. When plucked in a certain way and while standing under a rock formation shaped like a key lock, the notes transports the harpist to Hell. Within this Hell is an alien prison of one which has been occupied by Morbus for thousands of years.

Smith foolishly plucks some strings and inadvertently ends up down below, which is glowing with red fires everywhere. Bemoaning his fate, he begins to mutter about where he is and how he got there. **It is strange that whenever Smith ends up somewhere for some unexplainable reason he lets the viewers know how everything came to pass. Smith does a lot of babbling on** *Lost in Space,* **which sometimes is clever exposition of plot. And no one does it better than him. Once in awhile, after realizing his precarious predicament, he faints. This time he faints--but only after he finds a place to sit down.**

When he awakes, he is taken to a sparse yet plush room by Morbus whom Smith mistakes for the Devil. This is understandable because Morbus is wearing a bright red sequined outfit. Smith knows he is in Hell and that he deserves to be there, because Morbus shows him televised clips of his past which include a childhood, college and recent event. **The clips that Morbus shows are terrific, and Smith has never looked better than as a little boy snitch, a college boy thief, and a middle- aged glutton!** Trying to escape from Hell, he makes a deal with the alien prisoner, Morbus. The only way Morbus can be free of Hades is if someone breaks the harp, which is the key to unlocking the prison gate. **This won't be the first time that Smith makes a deal with the "Devil," but it's the first time he does it face to face.** Morbus wants Smith to destroy the harp in exchange for his freedom even though he doubts Smith can do it since the harp can only be broken by someone who is pure of heart. Nevertheless, he sends Smith back up to the surface of the planet. Smith ignores the robot's warning **(as usual)** about the alien and sneaks out to try to destroy the harp but is unsuccessful.

The next morning, the family sits down to an unappetizing looking breakfast of scrambled eggs. *Where the heck did Maureen get these eggs? I've never seen anything that looks like a chicken around here. All kind of monsters but never a chicken. I don't dare ask her what laid the eggs because she might tell me.* Judy suddenly gets up to go for a walk. She seems flustered, and Maureen follows her away from the table. Judy snaps at her about being old enough to go on a walk without being chaperoned and then leaves in a huff.

Don doesn't seemed concerned as he delves into the mystery egg concoction. *This tastes awful! Judy isn't missing anything. I just hope she gets over her mood by the time she gets back and doesn't pick up any stray animals on the way...or men.* **Don's thought, especially about men, becomes an o-men because Judy runs into Morbus and after a short flirtation brings him home.**

John gets up from the breakfast table to greet Morbus as if he were the next door neighbor. *What the hell is this?* **(Watch your language, Don. You could be hitting too close to home.)** *Judy is introducing us to a guy in a bright red spandex suit that even Santa wouldn't wear, and no one is questioning his being here? Maybe we've seen too many aliens, and they've become second nature to* *us now. He looks harmless enough.* A short time later, the robot's power pack explodes when it's asked a question about the new visitor. *He very definitely is an alien life form. What the hell else could he be?* **(There you go again!)**

Morbus takes Judy to the harp. Smith has taken control of it and stands near the rock formation shaped like a key lock. Smith again mistakenly plucks a cord with the transporting notes, but this time Morbus and Judy are transported below.

Smith returns to the campsite when he is accosted by Don after a restored robot **(restored by Will, of course)** revealed that Morbus has Judy with him in the underworld. *"Let me at him, John. Just this once! It won't take long. Give me two minutes alone with him. That's all I ask!!"* John threatens to leave Smith alone with Don unless he tells the entire story and brings them to the harp and key lock. **You can guess what Smith decided to do.** At the rock formation, they force Smith to play the transporting notes, and he is sent into the fiery underground again where he ends up in Morbus' prison room. Only this time, he is attacked by a monster. **I'm surprised Smith didn't try to eat him because he really resembled a spinach salad.** When fear overtakes Smith, he scurries away, dropping the harp as he goes.

Now that John and Don have heard the notes, they have the robot play them from memory and descend into Hell. Going in different directions, Don ends up in the room where Morbus and Judy are. Challenging "to bring it on," Don gets his dukes up and is ready to fight, except every time he swings Morbus disappears and ends up in a different place. *"Will you stay put, for crying out loud, so I can hit you!* "Judy comes to Don's aid and grabs the harp that Smith had dropped earlier. She tries to hit Morbus on the head but misses and instead knocks Don out cold. **Don can't win a fight no matter what the circumstances!** But, when the harp broke on Don's head, the gate to Hades opened because of Judy's purity of heart. **That purity that can only be matched in our next episode. So, to my Spanish speaking friends: I present to you from La Mas Famosa Serie de Ciencia Ficcion De Television Perdidos En el Espacio... "Castles in Space."**

"Castles in Space"

When introduced to Chavo, in "Castles In Space", I wondered if a knife wielding, sombrero wearing, widely grinning, guitar playing Mexican was a little stereotypical. I guess the writers feel that since he is painted silver and in space it makes a stereotypical character okay with our Spanish viewers. Whatever. At least Don gets a chance to be soft spoken in this episode yet firm and unrelenting when dealing with the bumbling Dr. Smith. Don soft spoken, you ask? Let's find out when and why.

The episode opens with Don working and Smith playing. **Now that's stereotypical!** Don, with Judy assisting below, is perched high on a radar tower, fixing an antenna. Smith is teaching Will how to skeet shoot with a slingshot and a rock. **That spells disaster.** *"Okay, Judy, that completes the task."* **Almost.** Smith fires the rock in Don's direction, and it hits Don, causing the radar tower to fall. **Don wasn't hurt but was lucky to escape injury.** *"Why, I outta... You know, Smith, I could get really angry right now, but because this could be such a nice campout for Will, Judy and me, I'll forget about how much I'd like to wring your scrawny neck. Just clean up the mess!"* Don and Judy leave for the campsite.

While cleaning up the mess and showing Will how to use a lever properly, Smith uncovers a solid block of frozen ice. There is some sort of a figure inside of it.

Will finds Don who tells Smith to guard whatever the block of ice contains. **Don trusts that Smith will be a good sentry. Sometimes the major just doesn't use common sense. But does anyone when it comes to Smith? At the cozy campsite, everything is copacetic.**

Don makes contact with John and tells him about the damaged tower and that the group would be at the site longer than expected. In turn, John tells Maureen, "I guess he knows what he's doing." **That is the best compliment paid to Don West since the journey began.** And the journey seems to be heading in the right direction as Don and Judy share a cup of coffee in this idyllic setting. **Wrong! I guess the moment was too heightened for our "romantic hero" because the next fireside scene has Will and Judy singing a duet while Don sleeps in his tent.** *Boy, if I could only play the guitar, I could be making time with Judy. Damn, it's cold up here. I could use some warming up besides this stupid thermal blanket. If Judy and I sleep with our fur parkas on, what harm could come of one little kiss? Ending up with a mouthful of fur, I guess. Who needs that? Go to sleep and stop torturing yourself. It's a beautiful night with soothing music, so what could go wrong? Smith? Even he can't turn a block of ice into a troubling situation.* **Wrong again, Don. Smith could turn a drop of water into Niagara Falls if he's not watched carefully.**

Smith's thermal blanket isn't warm enough for him, so he sheds it, tosses it aside and returns to the campsite for some coffee. He carelessly tossed the thermal blanket on the block of ice, and where once there was a figure, there is now the Princess Reyka. **The actress who plays Princess Reyka was Miss Greece and Miss Universe. She is quite beautiful but her character has the personality of a block of ice which I guess makes sense.** The princess comes to the campsite and threatens Smith with a spear made of ice which awakens everyone in the tents. *Whoa, what is this? She's really scared and wants to poke Smith with her spear. Maybe I should let her. It looks like it is made of ice and wouldn't make a dent in his cold heart.* **But because of Don's momentarily warm heart, he stops her from inflicting injury and calmly talks to her.** *"I'm sure you're as shocked to see us as we are to see you, except our shock is greater. You see, we are here because of natural evolution, not counting Dr. Smith, and you show up in a block of ice. That's what is shocking. But you're here and safe with us, so let me have that gigantic icicle and we can find out what this is all about."* Don is able to alleviate her fears.

Elsewhere, a ship arrives and Will sends the robot out to investigate. Poof...a metallic Mexican bandito appears. His name is Chavo. He immediately thinks the robot is a bull and wants to fight him. **That makes sense. A metallic looking Mexican bandito turning toreador against a metallic rotund robot.** On second thought, though, Chavo befriends the robot and gets it drunk on space Tequila. A drunken robot tells him about the princess. Chavo decides he wants to kidnap her for ransom, and a showdown at the O.K. Corral takes place when Don finds out Chavo's plans. Knives are the choice of weapons to be used and because Don is not "street wise", he loses. **This might have turned out differently if Don let Chavo have a knife and he used his laser rifle. The only problem was that earlier the bandito rendered the laser gun useless against his magic spell.**

Hearing of the plan, the Princess runs away. **The script should have done likewise.** Smith creates a dummy Mexican princess with the help of the robot to fool Chavo. This backfires and Smith is taken hostage, only to be released when the robot agrees to the bull-fight. To everyone's surprise, the bull wins! Chavo then decides the Princess isn't worth the bother and goes home. **Too bad, because if the MEXICAN Bandido had stayed around, he could have offered a shot of Tequila to *THE ANTI-MATTER MAN*.**

"The Anti-matter Man"

Considering all the *Lost In Space* episodes, of which one am I the most fond? For reasons of vanity, I like "The Anti-Matter Man." I think I look pretty good in a beard. Maybe I should have lived in Biblical times! Interesting sets and costumes along with excellent direction by Sutton Roley makes this a first class science fiction episode. Don gets to play an evil side of himself, so I decided to give him a rough beard and a scarred left eye. It seems to work for him. His evil self creates just the right amount of loathing and exasperation.

The story is the classic one of the good and evil that exist in all of us, taken to a height that only science fiction can explore. There is the evil John and the evil Don. These two criminals living in an anti-matter world need a transferral unit in order to contact their duplicates in an "other world." Coincidently, there is one on the planet where their duplicates live. In order to escape their dreaded world, they need to switch places with their duplicates.

While John and the robot are testing the Jupiter's atomic motors, they create a hole that draws John into the anti-matter universe. **Where is Don? This could have been more material for the "John and Don Show." Another screw up but this time the robot takes the place of Don. Get ready to keep track of a lot of "bads" and "goods".**

The bad John captures the good John, and they run into the bad Don, the duplicate of the good Don. He looks like Don except for a scarred left eye and a beard. **Why the scar and the beard? Beats me, but it makes the bad Don look tough and evil.** The good John, being dragged around by the bad John, asks the bad Don, "Who are you?" **The bad Don skips the formal introduction and tells the bad John, after he is told that the good John is the bad John's duplicate, "I want mine!" Still with me? Okay.** The Johns change clothes, and the good John is put into shackles. **What I love about this whole sequence, besides the music and spooky set, are the costumes. The arrangement of alternating white and black colors above and below the waist look "out of this world".** The bad John will do anything to escape, even kill if necessary.

In the real world, there is an electrical storm caused by the magnetic overlap of the two worlds. It is also happening in the negative world because two copies (the good and bad John) are the same person there.

Meanwhile, Will and the robot go back to the atomic motor, start it, and are transferred to the crossover point which is between dimensions. **Didn't anyone ever tell Will that "curiosity killed the cat"?** From there they are able to track John to the anti-matter world. In this new world, rocks can move but people can't. **Not good for rock climbing!** They run into the bad John, thinking he is the good John, and head back to the crossover point. **The crossover point is filmed with such imagination that it is visually some of the best photographic imagery on *Lost in Space*.**

All three return to the Jupiter 2. Once the bad John comes back to the real world as the good John, there is balance and all is calm. Everyone is happy to see him, but his manner is strange. He is rude to Maureen and is rather nasty when demanding that work has to be done in order to get ready for lift-off. Will notices that his watch is running backwards. *I'll be a son of a gun. My watch is running backwards, too.* Penny comes outside from the Jupiter and announces that the music on her machine is playing backward. *"That's a good way to listen to the Beatles, Penny. Just kidding!" What the heck is going on?* **You just don't get it, Don. The robot does. It recognizes that John doesn't cast a shadow, and therefore, is not the real John Robinson.** Will and the robot go to the crossover machine site to see if they can enter the "other world." The bad John unexpectedly shows up and beats the robot with an iron pipe, but

Will has already been successfully transferred. He is then followed by the bad John. Don and Smith bring the dazed robot to his tracks. **"Feet" doesn't work here, and how can anyone knock out a robot by hitting him on his metallic body? Whatever.** The robot is over his concussion and Don sends it to the anti-matter world. The bad John catches up to Will and tells him he will kill the good John if Will doesn't comply with his wishes to escape. **Now, the fun part for our bad Don West is about to happen.**

At the cave, a caged good John provokes the bad Don into losing his temper. **That's easy to do because the bad Don owns part of the good Don's questionable character traits. He has, as well, Don's inadequate fighting ability. He counters John with threats and anger.** *"Shut up...shut up!! I'll get my duplicate! I know it! Don't say I wont! He'll come back for me! He's not going to forget me! Stop saying that he won't come back!!... I outta..."* The bad Don starts banging the cage with chains as he yells at John. *"I'll get him! I'll kill him!"* Then the bad Don grabs a lighted torch. *I'll burn him, and he'll shut up! He's tricky like a monkey in that cage. I'll unlock the cage and open the barred door, so I can get at him! Now, I've got him. Just reach the torch in and burn him! Oops, he kicked me away. I'm falling. Damn! Too much good Don West in me, I guess.* The bad Don is knocked out.

John has better luck with his bad self. After the newly escaped good John catches up with the bad John on the crossover point between worlds, he knocks the bad John into an abyss that occupies neither world.

Afterwards, the real John Robinson, the robot and Will return to the ship. **All is well and balanced, except for the science of matter in the story. There isn't good and evil matter. Anti-matter is negative matter. When negative matter and normal matter come into contact, they destroy one another. As Einstein said E=MC2, but then again, Einstein never lived in a world where there could be the great vegetable rebellion.**

"The Great Vegetable Rebellion"

This is, Easily, the most talked about of all our Lost in Space *episodes*. Why, you ask? Even in the world of science fiction, some things are just plain unbelievably unbelievable. How do you talk to a carrot? Why do vines grow on the robot? Why does Penny blossom into flowers. How does Dr. Smith become a stalk of celery? How do serious actors keep from laughing when scenes turn into daffy comedic farce? I can only do my best to answer these questions as the show unfolds.

It's the robot's birthday. **Don, though, prefers to call it the robot's day of fabrication.** The family is throwing a party. *Boy oh boy, do I feel like a dork in this party hat. I can see Judy looking at me and thinking,*

"You look like such a dork in that party hat"! Oh, well, anything to make the family happy. Meanwhile, Jupiter 2 is orbiting a world of vegetation. Smith leaves the party but nobody notices right away. He takes the pod down to this world of vegetation to collect some flowers for the festivities. **Good decision, Smith. What's a birthday without flowers? That would be like an ice hockey game without ice! But, I'm sure Smith knows what he's doing.** When Smith cuts some flowers, there are tiny screams. Then, lo and behold, a giant carrot with an orange face appears and accuses him of killing innocent plants. Smith, of course, takes off. He runs into a character named Willoughby, who has been given a vegetable heart by the carrot man whose name is Tybo. When the carrot man catches up with Smith **(somehow, carrots can move really fast when necessary-- much faster than beets),** and he decides to turn the doctor into a vegetable. **I'm not sure what kind of vegetable I would want Tybo to turn Smith into, but I think I would choose one that can't be digested easily.**

When the family discovers that Smith is missing, John takes the Jupiter down to the planet. *"John, we can't go down to a place we know nothing about! What do you mean, we have to? What did you put into that birthday cake, Maureen? Just vanilla extract? Okay, let's go!"* The posse--John, Don, Maureen and Penny look for the pod while hacking their way through the jungle. *"John, stop! What's that I hear? You hear it, too? Yeah, like little screams. It's gone now."* They start hacking again. The screams return. *"John, you don't think...no, that's crazy!"* John and Don continue hacking away with dubious looks on their faces while the little screams continue. Maureen and Penny stop hacking and follow the men while grimacing all the time. As they advance through the flower vegetated jungle, they are suddenly trapped in a heavy cargo net. *What the heck is this? Where the hell did this come from?* **At this point, our posse of actors is trying to conceal their laughter while they move hesitantly under the smelly cargo net.**

In the meantime, that's not all that is going wrong. Back at the ship, the robot is attacked by vines that start to grow over it. Will and Judy are able free him, and the three of them set off to look for our incapacitated posse. The robot tells them that this is jungle warfare and that the jungle has declared war on human life. **The robot, somehow, must have a direct communication line to CNN.** They come across Smith, who is changing into a plant. **I'll bet Don wishes it were a poison ivy plant and he could watch while Smith itches himself to near death.** Then they are captured by some vines. Luckily, good old Willoughby shows up, talks to the vines, and they are released. **Nice guy, that Willoughby.**

After being transferred to a hot house, our posse is kept there by a force field. Willoughby comes to the rescue again, but he is too scared of the carrot man to help them escape. He does, however, tell them that there is a hydrostatic system under the hot house. *This seems like the perfect place to grow grass! And I don't mean the kind you mow. "Okay, John, I'm with you. Let's go below, but how do we get there? What?? Penny is turning into a plant? Is it a pretty plant, like her? I'm sorry, John, but some levity is necessary at times like this. Okay, it's not necessary. I said I was sorry. Jeeeeez."* John and Don find an unmarked trapdoor. **Those two fellows are very smart!** They enter the system. **Maybe not so smart, but very lucky.** They discover the water supply and shut it off. **Maybe, not so lucky, but very smart!** Plants can't grow without water, so Penny won't turn into a plant. **As if enough is not going on...**

Will and Judy fall into a pit where they are attacked by a weird looking plant, but the robot saves them. He then takes them to Smith who is becoming a stalk of celery. **How can Smith be saved and not end up in one of Maureen's delicious vegetable soups?** Will tries to talk Tybo, the carrot, into saving Smith but is unsuccessful. Fortunately, good old Willoughby shows up again and Judy talks him into curing Smith.

In the interim, the hot house has cooled off because of the quick thinking of John and Don. Without water, Tybo will die, but once the posse is set free, John, in his typical heroic fashion, gives him some water, saving his life.

Conclusion of *Three Years being Lost in Space*

In conclusion, I had a ball writing Mark and Don's "tongue in cheek" reminiscences about our time lost in space. Without the fans loyalty to the show and the encouragement of MGAS members, this endeavor never would have come to fruition. I only hope your time reading about the memories has been as enjoyable as my time writing about them.